His Other Son

His Other Son

A Novel

Ken Radon

Copyright © 2009 by Ken Radon.

Library of Congress Control Number: 2008911097
ISBN: Hardcover 978-1-4363-8904-4
Softcover 978-1-4363-8903-7

All rights reserved. No part of this book may be reproduced or transmitted in any form or by any means, electronic or mechanical, including photocopying, recording, or by any information storage and retrieval system, without permission in writing from the copyright owner.

This is a work of fiction. Names, characters, places and incidents either are the product of the author's imagination or are used fictitiously, and any resemblance to any actual persons, living or dead, events, or locales is entirely coincidental.

This book was printed in the United States of America.

To order additional copies of this book, contact:
Xlibris Corporation
1-888-795-4274
www.Xlibris.com
Orders@Xlibris.com

This is a work of fiction. All of the characters, organizations, locations, and events in this novel are either products of the author's imagination or are used fictitiously.

For my loving and supportive family, Melinda, Amy, Cameron, and Claire—you truly believe that anything and everything is possible.

And for my many friends and relatives who jokingly asked, "How did you write a book when you can't even read one?"

ACKNOWLEDGMENTS

I WANT TO offer a sincere thank you to a number of people for their invaluable assistance in the production of this book. First, my daughter, Amy Radon, who took the time and guided me through the entire writing process, patiently cleaned up one disaster after another. To Marilyn LeRud, who painstakingly edited my work, not once, but twice. To Bill Phillips, with the Pima County Sheriff's Department, who shared his law enforcement and technical expertise. To my wife, Melinda, who gave her constant support and encouragement. To Marian Lumayag, and the entire staff at Xlibris, who demonstrated diligence and professionalism throughout the entire publishing process. And finally, to my many friends and family members, who have enriched my life and were at times the inspiration behind the characters in this story. (Only the good guys!)

CHAPTER ONE

I DON'T REMEMBER ever having laughed . . . or cried. I don't believe that I have experienced true joy or emotional pain. I'm not certain that I have loved or been loved. And I do not understand concepts such as guilt, shame, compassion, embarrassment, sympathy, or empathy. I desperately want to be like others, able to experience these emotions. But I am who I am.

People say that I am gifted, although I have never accepted that label. I have what is called a true, photographic memory. Like a camera, my mind is able to take a picture of what my eyes see. I am then able to retrieve the exact images moments or even years later. Give me a ten-page document and two minutes, and I will be able to repeat the text verbatim. To me, this is not a gift but nothing more than a cheap trick, suitable for the stage or as a traveling carnival act.

I am fifty-two years old and the youngest of four children. Unlike me, my three brothers are all married with families, apparently happy, and all with very successful careers. My mother passed away almost thirty years ago, while my ninety-two-year-old father is in a nursing home and in rapidly failing health.

Growing up, Dad, like most fathers, enjoyed bragging about the accomplishments and exploits of his sons, from their academic achievements to their athletic undertakings. Dad indeed had a lot of reasons to boast. My three brothers were honor students and all-state athletes in a variety of sports. I was neither.

Dad rarely spoke of me, and when he did, he never used my name. Unable to accept responsibility for me or willing to claim ownership, to Dad, I was nothing more than *his other son*.

CHAPTER TWO

TUCSON IS A city of nearly eight hundred thousand people located in southeast Arizona. It sits equidistant from the state capitol of Phoenix to the north and its Mexican neighbor Nogales to the south, as both of these cities are an hour's drive away depending upon favorable traffic conditions on the interstate.

The Santa Cruz River no longer flows all year long as it did when the first pioneers arrived in the Old Pueblo and settled on its banks in the late 1600s. By the 1880s, Tucson was nothing more than a small town with a train stop, made somewhat famous by the escapades of such notorious gunfighters as Doc Holiday and Wyatt Earp. By comparison, Tombstone, about fifty miles to the southeast, was much more influential and populated.

By the 1950s, Tucson's population had reached about thirty thousand. With Davis-Monthan Air Force Base and Hughes Aircraft (founded by Howard Hughes and now known as Raytheon) as the leading employers, the inevitable development and rapid growth of the city had begun. As Tucson expanded east from the Santa Cruz River, which now only flows during the summer monsoons, the city planners in the 1950s decided, before it was too late, to set aside one square mile of land to be used for recreational purposes. Eventually Reid Park, named after a prominent

Tucson family, would become home to a zoo, two golf courses, the Cleveland Indians spring training facility Hi Corbett Field, numerous picnic areas, athletic fields, a tennis complex, and community center. In the 1960s and 70s, with the influx of midwesterners in search of a respite from the cold, Reid Park became surrounded by the expanse of the city—an emerald jewel in the middle of a rapidly growing metropolitan area.

The two golf courses in Reid Park were named after local dignitaries John Randolph and Dell Urich. Known as the Randolph Golf Complex, the courses share a pro shop, restaurant and bar, locker rooms, and practice facilities.

Today, most knowledgeable golfers agree that both Randolph and Dell are two of the finest municipal courses in the entire southwest. Each course has played host to the Tucson Open, and for years, they have been a favorite stop of the top professional golfers on the PGA and LPGA tours.

A bar and grill at a golf course is commonly referred to as "the 19th hole." After playing eighteen holes of golf, the 19th is a place where you can replenish your energy with anything from a bag of chips to a steak dinner, rehydrate, socialize with your playing partners, pay off gambling debts or collect your winnings, tell stories and lies, analyze the day's round, and in many cases, drown your sorrows.

Some golf courses try to come up with clever names for their 19th hole, such as, Mr. Putts, the Bogey Man, the Water Hole, Fairways, the Slice and Hook, and Shanks, just to name a few. The 19th hole at the Randolph Golf Complex has no such clever name. In fact, it has no name at all. It is simply referred to as "the Bar."

This simple description very much matches its utilitarian design and function. The large rectangular room, with seating for about sixty-five, has a somewhat worn gray industrial carpet dotted with many stains, and will probably be replaced in another year. Two small televisions are elevated and hung from the ceilings at both ends and are usually tuned to the Golf Channel. A rather small bar, roughly fifteen feet long, is positioned in the left rear corner of the room. Directly behind the bar is a small pass-through window leading to the kitchen where orders and food are routinely exchanged. There are no stools at the bar. Patrons simply stand to order their drinks and after being served, retreat to one of the roughly twenty tables to consume their beverages. Food is the only item delivered to the tables. A refill of any drink requires a repeat visit to the bar. Interestingly, there is a tip jar even though very little service is actually rendered. Back in the right rear corner of the room are two plain doors, one labeled M and the other W, which lead to the men's and women's locker rooms and their adjacent rest areas. The most attractive features of the Bar are the high wood-beamed ceiling and the entire front wall comprised of gigantic glass panels, which give an unobstructed view of much of the golf course and the Tucson Mountains to the west. Watching one of Tucson's renowned sunsets from the Bar is truly spectacular.

Although most people think of Tucson's climate as hot and dry, the middle of January usually finds the temperature at night dipping just below freezing, leaving a thin snow like sheet of frost on the fairways of the city's many golf courses. The sun rises at about 7:00 AM, and shortly thereafter, the frost is transformed into a light layer of dew. On this January morning, the Catalina Mountains to the north, with the light of day, would reveal a dusting of snow extending from the mountain's rugged peaks two-thirds of the way down to the homes in the foothills. The snow was placed there by a winter storm that passed by two days earlier.

Every employee at the Randolph Golf Complex wore a name tag with their first name and their state of birth. This included Sandy Wisconsin, who normally arrived at the Bar at 6:00 AM, still in the dark of night. The cook, Javier New Mexico, would not arrive until an hour later, but still early enough to get the kitchen up and running before the first patrons began to saunter in at about 7:30 AM. During her hour alone in the Bar each morning, Sandy would tidy up from the night before by wiping down the tables and bar, vacuuming the carpet, refilling the napkin and straw holders, and emptying the trash. By 8:00 AM, the Bar staff would be busy trying to keep up with a brisk breakfast business.

Sandy was a rather tall and ever so slightly overweight blonde with long hair that obviously took considerable time to set each morning. Her makeup may have been applied a tad generously, but the effect made her appear somewhat younger than her actual age of forty-four. It was clear she was a career waitress, learning the regulars by name and personally interacting with each customer while not appearing flirtatious. Although divorced, Sandy displayed a wedding band on her left hand primarily to discourage come-ons from any patron who may have had a pint too many.

There were two entrances leading into the Bar. The first faced south with a clear view of the complex's pro shop across a small putting area and along a short concrete walkway. The second entrance was to the north, conveniently located just off the ninth green of Randolph for golfers who needed a midround pick-me-up on their way to the tenth tee. As Sandy approached the southern door, the security light from the pro shop emitted enough light to show that something had gone terribly awry in the time since the Bar had closed, without incident, the night before. Broken glass was scattered all over the exposed aggregate walkway leading up to the door, which caused Sandy to slow her characteristically brisk gait, until she reached the first shards of glass. There, she was brought to a complete halt, the result of both fear and apprehension.

Over the past nine years, Sandy had opened the Bar to find that it had been broken into on only two occasions. Because the money from the cash register was routinely dropped into a safe each night, the only losses in each of these break-ins were a few bottles of booze and damage from minor vandalism. The perpetrators in each of these instances were never apprehended.

But Sandy could sense that this was different. The broken glass was strewn on the walkway outside the Bar, while the glass from the previous burglaries had been scattered inside. Instead of entering the southern door, which was now little more than an empty frame, Sandy decided to make her way along the glass-paneled front of the Bar to the northern entrance, keeping her eyes glued to the shadows behind those panels and searching for any potential trouble. Since she saw nothing out of the ordinary during her slow and steady trek between the Bar's entrances, she nervously unlocked the northern door. With a racing heart, she slowly opened the door and reached her trembling hand inside, groping for the light switches that were located on the wall. The three switches, each of which illuminated a different section of the Bar, were turned on simultaneously with the brush of Sandy's rather large right hand.

Sandy had seen a lot in her forty-plus years. Although probably considered somewhat tough, her past life experiences had never prepared her for this gruesome sight. The contorted body of a man laid motionless on the tattered carpet, covered and lying in a pool of blood. A golf club was buried into his skull with the shaft sticking out at a forty-five-degree angle. Fragments of the victim's cranium were on the floor in close proximity to the head, while a section of brain had oozed from the wound. Having not eaten since the previous night, Sandy managed to dry heave small amounts of bile as she raced next door to the pro shop in search of help.

CHAPTER THREE

PETE IOWA, THE assistant pro, normally arrived at the pro shop at 7:00 AM. His multifaceted job, which often resulted in a sixty-hour-work week, included record and bookkeeping, ordering clothing and golf equipment for the pro shop, scheduling events, overseeing the facility's maintenance, coordinating tee times and employee supervision, to name a few. During the Christmas holidays, he had taken time off to visit family and friends back in his hometown of Des Moines, which now required him to arrive an hour early each day until he caught up with his backlog of work. Pete had just fired up the coffeemaker in his tiny cluttered office when the electronic buzzer on the pro shop door alerted him to the fact that someone had entered. Because Pete had not been expecting anyone for at least another hour, he was mildly startled and accidentally knocked a teetering stack of papers off his desk and onto a box of new Titleist golf clubs that had arrived a day earlier. As he left his office and entered the retail area of the pro shop, he was surprised to see his somewhat winded and visibly shaken friend, Sandy, from the Bar.

Pete and Sandy had developed a very friendly relationship without any risk of intimacy. At twenty-eight years old, Pete was considerably younger than Sandy. Additionally, he had been happily married for two years, and with an infant at home, there was little time left during the day for any extra curricular activities, even if he were interested. Sandy, on the other hand, preferred older men, though the sting of her divorce three years earlier lingered and left her uninterested in any type of relationship.

Nevertheless, Pete and Sandy were kindred spirits. Their common bonds were that each of their lives had taken unexpected turns and each had come to realize, at different points, that many of their unfulfilled dreams would remain just that.

Pete was the 1998 state golf champion as a senior at Des Moines Central High School. He went to Iowa State on a golf scholarship and earned All American honors his final two seasons. Upon graduation, he pursued his dream of earning a living, competing as a touring golf professional. Although he was a very accomplished golfer, the competition on the small satellite tours was incredible. He was barely able to eke out a meager existence eating burgers, sleeping in his car, and showering in the men's locker rooms of the venues at which he played. During the off-season from October to March, he worked in his father's furniture store back home in Des Moines. Pete was a tall man, standing just a smidge under six foot four. After three years on the tour, he began to develop chronic back pain, undoubtedly exacerbated by sleeping in the back of his Honda Civic. Encouraged, or discouraged depending on perspective, by his high school sweetheart and now his wife, he abandoned his dream of competitive golf after two more painful seasons.

The job as an assistant club pro paid his young family's bills. Except for the occasional lesson, likely to someone the head golf pro did not want to deal with, it was basically an unglamorous management position that required selling overpriced shirts, shoes, clubs, and balls to golfers who could purchase the same items considerably cheaper elsewhere. Pete was also learning from the head pro all aspects of golf course management, and with a few more years of this apprenticeship, he would be able to begin applying for those positions. Though Pete was paid well, becoming the head pro at a golf course would be the extent of his possible vertical career advancement.

Sandy's dreams were much simpler and ended when her sterile husband of eighteen years left town to, as he said, "find himself." Later she discovered that he had companionship on his journey. Sandy had desperately wanted children, but at forty-four, her biological clock was no longer ticking.

"My god, Sandy, what's wrong?" Pete asked his out-of-breath friend who had flown from the Bar to the pro shop.

Crying and almost hysterical, Sandy replied, "There's a guy on the floor next door covered in blood . . . he's dead."

As soon as the words left her mouth, she dry vomited again as she pictured the horrible sight in her mind. Pete calmly dialed 9-1-1 and began to comfort his friend, but not before checking out the scene inside the Bar for himself.

CHAPTER FOUR

IT TOOK THE first responders less than three minutes to arrive at the Randolph Golf Complex. Pete, along with Sandy, who by now had regained her composure, met the two police officers in the parking lot just outside of the pro shop.

"Is everyone here OK?" Badge 803 asked no one in particular.

"We're the only two here except for the dead guy in the Bar," quipped Sandy, not wanting to sound glib, but realizing she had.

"Ma'am, how do you know he's dead?" queried Badge 119, with his breath visible in the chilly morning air.

As the visual image returned, Sandy, who was trying to be helpful said, "He's on the floor, there's blood everywhere, his eyes are staring wide open," and as her voice began to quiver, added, "and there's a golf club sticking out of his head."

Badge 803 confirmed the location of the body with Sandy and having been in the Bar before, went to see for himself what Sandy had described. He told his partner and the two visibly shaken golf course employees simply to, "Wait here."

Upon returning a few moments later, Badge 803 looked directly at Pete and assuming he was the one in charge, asked, "How many ways are there in and out of this complex?"

"This is the only way in," answered Pete, pointing behind himself to the two large rusted wrought iron gates.

"And oh," he added, "there is the entrance for the ground crew over on the other side of the golf course, off of Country Club Road."

Just then, a second police car pulled up behind the first. Badge 803 left Pete and Sandy with Badge 119 at the curb and walked over to the second set of officers, instructing them to secure the Country Club Road entrance. "We have a murder scene," he told them. "No one in or out." The officers in the second police car immediately sped off to attend to their task.

Badge 803, in an attempt to convey knowledge and authority, returned to Sandy and Pete and explained to them the policemen's job as first responder. They were to check on the welfare of the civilians at the scene and render aid if necessary. Then, they were to secure the crime scene to prevent the contamination of any of the evidence. While he spoke, Badge 119 had grabbed a roll of yellow crime scene tape from the car and was carefully stringing it back and forth from the posts of the wrought iron gate, leaving the gate itself untouched and in the open position.

"Now we have to wait for the crime scene unit and the homicide detectives to arrive. They will take over the investigation," said Badge 803, sounding disappointed. It was apparent to Sandy and Pete that he would have enjoyed taking command of this situation.

"The only other thing I need you to do is contact your supervisors." He added, "The detectives are going to need their help too."

Pete used his cell phone to call the head pro, and then handed it to Sandy who called the manager of the Bar.

Within the next ten minutes, no less than eight additional police cars arrived. Although there was a lot of standing around, the massive police presence conveyed that what had happened was significant and was being taken very seriously.

It was only about 6:45 AM, and the very first hints of daylight were beginning to appear. Along Alvernon Way, the traffic became heavier as the early risers began their morning commute. Drivers slowed as they rubbernecked at the unusual sight of all the police cars in the parking lot of the Randolph Golf Complex. Farther to the east, the dark silhouette of the Rincon Mountains looked like ominous storm clouds on the horizon.

It had been just slightly less than an hour since Sandy's horrific discovery, yet it seemed much longer. Pete and Sandy realized almost simultaneously that it was extremely cold that morning. Unable to re-enter the complex because of the yellow tape, Pete volunteered to hike across the parking lot and Alvernon Way to the Circle K convenience store for two hot coffees.

They both knew it was going to be a long day.

CHAPTER FIVE

MIKE GROMAN KNEW that a phone call before his alarm clock sounded was never a good thing.

"Son of a bitch," he muttered to himself as he knocked over a glass on the nightstand next to his bed while fumbling in the dark for his cell phone. Mike was mildly hung over from his monthly poker game that had ended just a few hours earlier, making this task more difficult than it needed to be. The commotion awakened his wife of thirty years, Jeanie, who was slightly annoyed that this was now the second time in one night that her peaceful slumber had been interrupted. After finally finding his phone and silencing its piercing ring, Mike listened while half asleep to the voice on the other end and after about a minute quietly said, "I'll be right there."

This was the life of the captain of the homicide unit for the Tucson Police Department, the TPD.

Mike's clock registered 6:45 AM, and he sorely missed the extra fifteen minutes of sleep he would have had if not for the call. Gaining his senses as he sat on the edge of the bed, his hangover was amplifying the slightest sounds, including the automatic coffee maker, which had just started in the kitchen. After a shower and shave, he quickly dressed and was out the door, but not before grabbing a breakfast bar and filling his large insulated thermos with freshly brewed coffee.

Mike Groman was a hulk of a man, standing six-feet-six-inches tall and weighing 270 pounds. This was also his exact size forty years earlier when he was a star high school football player in Red Bluff, California. He had numerous scholarship offers to play college football at schools across the country, including Cal, USC, and Ohio State. Unable to qualify academically to a four-year school, he decided to go to Scottsdale Community College, where he could play football and work on his academic standing. After that, he moved on to Northern Arizona University where he played two more years of college ball, and then was drafted by the Cleveland Browns in the thirteenth round of the 1974 draft. He played one year of professional football until his final knee injury ended his very brief career.

Mike, however, had a back up plan. He had graduated with a bachelor's degree in criminal justice before departing for Cleveland, so after his injury, he decided to return to Arizona to pursue a career in law enforcement. In 1976, he joined the Tucson Police Department as a patrolman and over the next twenty years, slowly moved up the ranks until he was named captain of the homicide unit, a position that demanded only the best and the brightest. Although he had more than enough years of service for retirement, the fact of the matter was that he loved his job and was very good at it. He was not looking forward to mandatory retirement, which loomed just four years down the road.

Mike's football career had taken a toll on his body. Within a span of eight years, he had five surgeries that replaced both hips, both knees, and finally his left shoulder. The last operation was in 2006, and for the first time in decades he was pain free, although he walked with a clear limp. His friends jokingly referred to him as the bionic man.

Captain Groman, as he was known to the TPD's regular patrolmen, had a presence about him, so when he arrived at the Randolph Golf Complex everyone knew that he was in charge. His five detectives, who would arrive later that morning, more casually called him Mike.

The sun was now up over the Rincon Mountains, revealing a sky that was void of clouds. The traffic along Alvernon Way was now bumper-to-bumper yet moving steadily, as cars slowed to observe the adjacent parking lot that was scattered with police cars. Two police officers had set up a barricade at the lone entrance to the parking lot, turning away disappointed golfers with a brief explanation of what had happened.

It was now 8:15 AM as Mike approached Sandy, Pete, the head golf pro Don Nebraska, who had arrived just moments earlier, and a dozen or so other police officers.

"What's the situation?" Mike asked, while panning the group to see who would step up and answer.

"My partner and I took the call and were the first to arrive on the scene at about 6:15," said a somewhat intimidated Badge 803, who nervously moved to the front of the group, but eager to impress the captain.

At this time, Mike Groman removed a small spiral notebook from his pocket and began taking notes.

Badge 803 continued, "This is Pete, the assistant pro that phoned it in, and this is Sandy—she discovered the body."

Without looking up, Mike asked, "Do Pete and Sandy have last names?"

Feeling sheepish that he had not taken the time to learn the witnesses' full names, Badge 803 groped for words as he turned to Pete Iowa, who took the cue and said, "I'm Pete Federer, that's F-E-D-E-R-E-R, and this is Sandy with a *y*. Her last name is Anklin, A-N-K-L-I-N."

Mike looked over the top of his glasses in their direction, now associating names with faces.

"It's nice to meet you folks," Mike said somewhat insincerely.

Realizing it was time for introductions, and not wanting to be left out, Don added without prodding, "and I'm Don Weber, the head pro. That's Weber with one *b*, just like the barbeque grill." This was the same line Don had used hundreds of times with no one ever amused.

With the introductions now out of the way, Captain Groman dismissed all of the policemen at the scene except Badges 803 and 119, the first responders.

Turning to Pete, Sandy, and Don, Mike said, "I'll be with you folks shortly," making it clear that they were not dismissed.

With a head gesture toward Badge 803, Mike said, "Show me what we've got." The two walked together to the wrought iron gate and ducked through the yellow crime scene tape. Badge 803 did so with ease, while

Mike had some difficulty. His flexibility was limited by the hour of the morning, the chilly desert air, and his numerous replacement parts.

As they walked slowly toward the Bar, Mike took in the sights and sounds as if he was trying to glean useful information or clues from the surroundings. Badge 803 was afraid to interrupt the captain's train of thought but broke the uneasy silence when they arrived at the Bar by saying, "This is the worst I've seen." Badge 803 was not a rookie—he was well into his eighth year on the force and had seen plenty.

The Tucson Crime Scene Unit, or TCSU as it is referred to by those in law enforcement, had not yet arrived when Badge 803 began showing Mike the scene inside the Bar. As a result, both men were very careful not to touch or step on anything that could possibly be considered as evidence. They followed the same path that Sandy had taken earlier, by first going to the shattered south door and then proceeding along the large glass panels to the unlocked north door. After putting on a latex glove, Mike carefully opened the door and took one step inside. From there, he could view the entire room, including the body of the victim on the floor. Badge 803 remained outside.

Once again, Mike pulled out the spiral notebook and took copious notes for the next fifteen minutes. Badge 803 was curious as to what he had jotted down in his notebook, but wisely chose not to ask when Mike finally exited the Bar. Seemingly unaffected by what he had seen, Mike, in a matter-of-fact tone, simply said, "Let's go back out front."

CHAPTER SIX

PETE, SANDY, DON, and Badge 119 were now joined by a cast of new characters. The TCSU van had arrived, carrying three technicians and their high-tech, space-aged equipment.

The TCSU's downtown crime lab, where evidence from each crime scene is carefully analyzed and cataloged, is a state-of-the-art facility. Local federal agents, who occasionally use the laboratory, favorably compare it to the FBI's crime lab in Quantico, Virginia, though it is somewhat smaller. Most of the crime lab was paid for by a generous grant from the Department of Homeland Security. Tucson's close proximity to Mexico makes it a vulnerable avenue for illegal entry into the country. Although most border crossers are Mexican nationals simply in search of work, those with a more sinister intent, such as drug runners and terrorists, have been known to tempt fate by crossing the smoldering desert to meet up with those on the other side. The ability of this unit to gather and process evidence quickly and accurately is a tremendous law enforcement advantage.

Back at the scene, Mike Groman's five homicide detectives had arrived nearly at the same time as the TCSU and were huddled together, lamenting the University of Arizona's overtime loss to Washington State in basketball the night before. Each had their own take on the debacle, ranging from bad calls by the officials, terrible coaching, wrong substitutions, or the particularly poor play of one player or another. Tucsonans take their basketball very seriously.

Mike felt that each murder scene had what he called "a signature." What he meant was that with a cursory inspection of the scene, coupled with general knowledge of the area, he could reasonably predict if the homicide was gang, drug, or domestic in nature.

While Mike's five detectives worked as a team, each specialized in one of these specific types of homicides. For each murder, Mike would assign one of his detectives to be the lead, according to the type of homicide and the detective's specialty, while the others would serve as the lead's assistants.

As captain of the homicide unit, Mike Groman answered only to the chief of police, George Sladec. Mike's job was primarily administrative, although he occasionally handled the high profile cases, usually at the request of the chief. Mike knew shortly after arriving on the scene that this would become one of those cases. Like a football coach with a game plan, Mike had already outlined his strategy and the direction the investigation would need to go. He also knew that his already overworked team would not be able to help with this investigation without sacrificing the quality of work on their individual cases, and that he did not want.

Just as Mike's detectives had wrapped up their basketball conversation and were starting to wonder where their leader had ventured, Mike and Badge 803 reappeared and climbed back through the yellow crime scene tape. The idle chatter in the parking lot ended as everyone knew it was time to get to work. Before reaching the group, Mike abruptly stopped as he pulled out his cell phone and said to Badge 803, "Go on over and tell them I'll be right there."

Much like a caterpillar metamorphoses into a butterfly, a freezing night in Tucson becomes a balmy day with just a few hours of sunlight. Mike removed his coat, revealing a blue button-down oxford shirt, a solid burgundy tie with a Polo logo and a pair of neatly pressed gray slacks. Mike's clothing fit him well, as he appeared fit without any signs of an extra tire despite his large frame.

Mike waited patiently with his cell phone pressed against his ear until he finally said, "Good morning, George, its Mike."

After a short conversation, the chief of police ended the call by saying, "They're yours. I'll set it up. Anything else you need, let me know."

CHAPTER SEVEN

MIKE WALKED WITH a purposeful stride toward the waiting assembly in the parking lot. It was shortly after 9:00 AM, and the traffic on Alvernon Way had eased considerably from the rush of an hour earlier. A set of A-10 jets from Davis-Monthan Air Force Base, flying low and in a tight formation, were banking hard directly overhead. Mike looked annoyingly toward the sky as he waited for their thunder to subside.

"It's all yours," he finally said, looking directly at the trio from the TCSU. They were dressed smartly in one-piece navy blue jumpsuits with their names embroidered on the front. After receiving the go-ahead from Captain Groman, they grabbed their equipment and briskly walked toward the Bar, revealing the letters *TCSU* in large, golden block print on their backs.

Mike corralled his five detectives and separated them from Pete, Sandy, Don, and Badges 803 and 119. Out of earshot from the others, he said, "Guys, this is going to be my case." Each detective understood that these were the code words for "high profile" and were somewhat relieved that this case was not going to be added to their already-full platters.

"Anything we can do," said Dave Starbuck, Mike's second in command, "just let us know." After vowing their support, the five were dismissed to get back to their own investigations.

"Who shut down the Bar last night?" Mike asked, after he returned to the remaining five.

"That was Donna Fulton," said Sandy, knowing that Captain Groman wanted full names. "She's also the manager."

"Why isn't she here?" Mike asked with a slightly scolding tone.

Badge 803, attempting to abdicate any responsibility, chimed in, "I asked her to call when we first arrived," while gesturing toward Sandy.

Now on the defensive, Sandy said, "I've called twice and left a message each time on her voice mail. I told her it was urgent and to call right away."

With nothing left to discuss on this issue, Mike said politely, "Please try again."

Without saying a word, Pete once again handed Sandy his cell phone. For a third time, she was unsuccessful in reaching Donna, although she left yet another message before handing the phone back to Pete.

Don seized the opportunity of a slight pause in the conversation to ask, "Can you tell me when you think we might be able to open for business?"

"You should be good to go tomorrow," answered Mike. "But the Bar is going to be closed for some time. They've got to clean it up and replace the carpeting."

The last sentence had a chilling effect on Don, who for the first time realized the magnitude of the horrendous scene inside the Bar. He was now ashamed that he callously asked about opening for business.

Just then, Pete's cell phone sounded, chiming to the tune of "When the Saints Go Marching In," a lively ditty, which contrasted sharply with the overall somber mood of the group. Donna, the manager of the Bar, finally received Sandy's messages. Pete wasted no time with the gruesome details, instead opting for a succinct summary of the morning's events. "There was a dead guy in the Bar when Sandy opened up this morning, and the cops want you to come in right now." Donna told Pete she was on her way.

"She'll be here in about twenty minutes," Pete said to Captain Groman, who had figured it was Donna who had just called.

"Great," said Mike approvingly. "Until she gets here, why don't you folks have a seat over on the bench," he said, gesturing toward two concrete benches located close to the curb that young golfers used while waiting for their rides.

Mike now turned his full attention to Badges 803 and 119 said, "We need to talk."

CHAPTER EIGHT

WHEN MIKE GROMAN asked Chief of Police George Sladek if he could temporarily reassign Badges 803 and 119 to his unit, it was not an unusual request. The Tucson Police Department had an ever-shrinking budget due in part to the city's large population of fixed income retirees who would vote down any measure that would raise taxes. As a result, the constant shifting of personnel to handle urgent needs was a routine practice.

Whether instinctively or intuitively, Mike always had the unique ability to quickly and accurately judge people and their character. This skill served him well in life and particularly as a detective. It did not take him long to form a favorable opinion of the two patrolmen he met for the first time that morning.

"If it's OK with you," Mike said to both badges, "I would like to temporarily assign you to my unit to help me with this investigation," pausing to add the qualifier, "if you feel you are up to it." Mike knew that this proposal was a mere formality, knowing that any patrolman would jump at this plum opportunity. Badge 803 glanced ever so quickly at his excited partner, and then answered, "Count us in."

Badge 803 was actually Floyd LeRud, the senior partner of the two and an eight-year veteran of the force. He was thirty-five years of age, although he looked much younger. Lean and fit without appearing gaunt, he religiously worked out five days a week at his health club. Floyd was single and had never been married—in fact, the longest of his many relationships had lasted less than six months. His twelve-dollar haircut and overall grooming, while clean and neat, suggested he never embraced metrosexuality.

Professionally, Floyd was a very skilled officer and was able to display a kaleidoscope of personas depending upon which would best facilitate the desired outcome of any given situation. He took his job seriously, was a quick learner, followed directions well, and was never afraid to take the initiative. These were all traits that Mike Groman would come to appreciate.

Badge 119 was Ray Schrader, who learned everything he knew about law enforcement from his partner, Floyd. He was still somewhat of a rookie having joined the force only two and a half years ago. He was a competent officer, although he lacked the confidence that comes with years of experience. Affable and with good instincts, he would one day probably develop into an outstanding officer. Ray's strong suits were his bulldog determination and attention to detail, the latter trait being his partner's weakest. As a result, the two made for a very good team.

Ray was small in stature at five feet six inches, and while standing next to Mike Groman, the pair resembled Mutt and Jeff. Wiry and with an accelerated metabolism, Ray was able to consume large quantities of food and never gained an ounce. That fact constantly annoyed Floyd, who had to work diligently at weight maintenance. Ray was single, but his girlfriend of two years had recently moved in, and the two were talking of marriage, possibly as early as November.

The two officers who were manning the barricade to the parking lot had just let the coroner's vehicle slip past. If the Grim Reaper were to drive, this would be his means of transportation. The late model Cadillac hearse had an ominous and foreboding appearance—it would never be associated with a joyous occasion. Long and solid black, including the tint on the windows, it was meticulously spit and polished. The only intrusion on what appeared to be a solid onyx gemstone was the four-inch white lettering that spelled "CORONER." The driver lowered the window and after a brief conversation with Captain Groman, pulled the hearse in front of Sandy, Pete, and Don, who were still waiting patiently on the concrete bench. They watched silently as the occupants of the vehicle exited and grabbed a gurney from the rear and proceeded toward the Bar.

Donna Fulton finally arrived and was permitted past the barricade just as the coroner had done moments earlier. She was wearing her name tag, "Donna West Virginia," along with the same clothing from the night before. Frequently, Donna would not find her way home, choosing instead to explore the bedrooms of different men.

It was now close to 11:00 AM, and the once totally blue sky was beginning to yield to a number of thick, puffy clouds. The local evening news stations had predicted rain for the next day, and it looked like it was going to arrive on schedule.

Mike, with Floyd LeRud and Ray Schrader now at his side, strode over to meet with the four golf course employees—Sandy, Pete, Don, and Donna.

"Is there a way we can get a list of anyone that stepped foot on this property yesterday?" Mike asked, inferring that everyone was a suspect.

Pete responded first, offering, "I can get the names of everyone that paid for golf or purchased anything from the pro shop and used a credit card." Because a round of golf cost forty-seven dollars, many chose to use their charge cards. "We also have the names of anyone that made a reservation, even if they paid cash. The only golfers we would not have a record of would be anyone that walked on to fill the place of a no-show golfer and paid cash, but we get very few of them."

Tucson in January is a mecca for midwesterners who seek relief from their harsh winter. Unsurprisingly, golf courses fill out rapidly and tee times are prized possessions, which sometimes require a reservation made weeks in advance.

"That's great," said Captain Groman, feeling for the first time that the investigation was finally and officially underway.

Don jumped in and offered a list of all the employees that had worked that day. His help was also welcomed.

Sandy, sensing it was her turn to contribute said, "Almost everyone in the Bar pays cash, but I'll get the few credit card receipts that we have."

"That'll be fine," said Mike.

Now looking at Donna, Mike said, "I understand from talking to Sandy that you closed the Bar last night."

"I did, but I don't know anything," said Donna, imagining a subtle accusatory tone.

"I know you probably don't, but the fact of the matter is that *if* you left the Bar last night and everything was fine, how did a guy end up dead on the floor when Sandy arrived to open up this morning?"

Now appreciating Mike's quandary, Donna said, "I understand what you're saying, and I'm willing to help, but I thought I was being accused of something I know nothing about."

"Listen, Ms. Fulton," Mike said sternly, "I'm not the most subtle guy. If I was accusing you of something, trust me, you'd know it."

Donna, now somewhat intimidated and realizing that her small outburst was unjustified, offered a brief apology. "I'm sorry. I had a bad night. What can I do to help?"

Mike then softened his stance and directed Donna to Officers LeRud and Schrader and said, "You could really help if you would sit down with these two officers and give them a step by step detailed account of everything you did last night from approximated 5:00 PM until you walked out the door and locked up. Leave nothing out, no matter how small a detail. Go over it again and again. The slightest detail may be important." As the three walk to the concrete bench to begin their task, Mike noticed that Donna was paying particular attention to Ray's firm ass.

Once again, Mike turned his attention back to Sandy, Pete, and Don. "Those lists will have to wait until tomorrow. The crime scene unit will be in there all day." Looking up at the thickening clouds, Mike added, "It's supposed to rain tomorrow . . . good day to work on those lists. I'll pick them up sometime around noon." Mike thought it was always important to set a strict time frame for fact-finding and also wanted to indicate to these three that this potentially important information was needed sooner, rather than later.

Mike then dismissed Pete and Don and gave his full attention to Sandy. He took down her detailed statement, documenting every move she made when she arrived in the morning. When she was done, he sent her on her way as he had done with the others.

By noon, Donna had finished giving her statement and was also dismissed. Mike looked approvingly over the work of Floyd and Ray and suddenly realized that his two new investigators, who had normally worked the night shift, had been on the job for over twelve hours.

Although it was only a shade past noon, Mike said, "You guys have had a long day. Get a good night sleep and be in at 8:00 AM sharp. Lose the uniforms—sport coats and slacks will do. No tie."

Before leaving, Floyd, who was still on a rush of adrenaline, asked, "Captain, how long until they ID the victim?"

Mike responded, "Usually when the CSU moves the body for the first time, they will check to see if he has a wallet, in which case they will know right away who he is. If not, it can sometimes take a while."

Then he shocked Floyd and Ray by saying, "This time it doesn't matter. His name is Nick Trikilos."

Mike Groman remained at the crime scene until later that afternoon when the coroner tentatively identified the victim and removed the body. The Pima County sheriff's office located Andreas Trikilos, the victim's brother and after informing him of Nick's death, escorted him to the morgue to make a positive identification. This was all standard procedure and except for the coroner's report, would be the extent of the county's involvement in this case.

The local NBC, ABC, and CBS news affiliates each aired a brief story on the 5:00 PM news that evening, reporting that "the body of an unidentified sixty-year-old white male has been discovered at the Randolph Golf Complex," and added that "the victim's name and cause of death will not be released until the next of kin have been notified." By the 10:00 PM news later that night, the victim's name was given along with a brief description that Nick Trikilos was a local businessman and that the cause of death was being ruled a homicide.

CHAPTER NINE

KILLING NICK TRIKILOS did not go as I had planned. This was my first murder, after all, and maybe I should have anticipated some problems. When we completed our round of golf, I expected to follow him out into the parking lot and finish him off with one swift blow to the head with one of my golf clubs. He surprised me, instead, when he suggested that our foursome should go into the Bar and have a few beers, to which everyone quickly agreed.

After our second pitcher, the other two members of our group had to leave. Suddenly, I was alone with my target, who had grown tired of beer and had switched to bourbon. I tried to encourage Nick to leave, but he was intent on telling me one story after another. The more he drank, the more he talked. All the while, I was slowly nursing my beer, as I needed to keep my wits about me.

It was around seven o'clock and near closing when Nick asked me to help him to the men's room, as by now he could barely walk. The entrance to the men's room, and the adjoining locker room, was located at the rear of the Bar. Nick relieved himself and then splashed cold water on his face in a futile attempt to sober up. Failing to do so, he realized that he was in no condition to drive home. He reached into his pocket and handed me his cell, then asked me to call him a cab, using the number from his directory. I got the impression that Nick often called for a ride under similar circumstances.

Nick was seated next to me on a bench in the men's locker room as I pretended to make the call. Then, a woman, who I assumed was our waitress, poked her head inside the doorway and called out to see if the locker room was empty. I panicked. I grabbed Nick and firmly held my hand over his mouth to silence him, should he have tried to call out. It worked. He could not make a sound and offered very little resistance. Assuming the locker room was empty, the woman turned off the lights and left.

I sat with my hand over Nick's mouth for what seemed like an hour. Then, I put him in a headlock and dragged him back out into the now empty and dark lounge.

At this point, I could understand Nick's slurred words as he said, "I want to go home."

I grabbed him by the collar of his shirt and the back of his trousers and said, "You want to go home? Then let's go home."

With that, I ran him head first into the glass door leading out from the Bar. The door seemed to explode upon impact. Half of Nick's body remained inside while the other half was lying outside on the concrete walkway leading up to the door. I grabbed him by his ankles and dragged him back inside the Bar, where I planned on finishing him off if he was not already dead. I observed him for a few moments, bleeding profusely from his head and lying as if frozen on the floor. I went back into the locker room and retrieved my clubs from where I had stored them while we were drinking. I returned to the Bar to find Nick still face down and motionless, though now I could distinguish some faint moans. I grabbed my seven iron and with a number of swift blows to the head, I ended the life of Nick Trikilos. I then took my golf bag and climbed through the broken door and left the vacant golf complex undetected.

I have never intentionally hurt another person, much less killed one. Although the murder of Nick Trikilos did not go as I had expected, he was dead nonetheless. By the next morning, I was on my way to California, where I needed to be by Friday. There, I hoped my next murder would go according to plan.

CHAPTER TEN

WHILE CAPTAIN MIKE Groman was driving to work in a downpour the following morning, the signature of this murder occupied his thoughts. Mike knew that this was not a gang, drug, or domestic homicide that his unit regularly investigated. This murder was different—more sinister and depraved. This was revenge. This was payback. This was personal.

Mike's thoughts were suddenly interrupted by Dave "Muddy" Waters, the morning DJ on his oldies radio station KTZU, the Zoo. Mike listened to this station exclusively and had done so for eight years after the station dropped its country/western format. It was Thursday, 7:45 AM, and Muddy Waters was about to do his weekly "tribute to the workingman." Muddy would choose an occupation and then cleverly select and play three songs that somehow related to that occupation, sans commercial interruption. He did this routine on Thursday morning instead of Friday to ensure his listening audience would be at its largest because as he always said, "No one in Tucson works on Friday." This week, he singled out his friends in law enforcement. The first selection was "The Man Who Shot Liberty Valance" by Gene Pitney, followed by the Sam Cooke classic, "Chain Gang." As Mike pulled into the parking lot of the police station, the final song of the trilogy, "I Fought the Law (and the Law Won)" by the Bobby Fuller Four, had just started playing. Mike listened intently, joined in on the chorus, and noticed that the clicking of his windshield wiper kept perfect time with the rhythm of the song.

When the song ended, Mike raced through the parking lot as quickly as his replacement knees and hips could carry him. He considered the use of an umbrella to be somehow feminine and instead opted for the "head duck" method of keeping dry, as if that ever worked.

Once inside the station, Mike was greeted with a loud and cheerful, "Good morning, Captain," by Sergeant Anaya who was manning the front desk.

"Morning," answered Mike, declining to indicate whether it was indeed good or otherwise. The two had repeated this exact same exchange ritualistically every morning for years.

Mike made a hard left, traveled down a long hallway and entered the last room on the right. A simple sign above the door read Rm. 144—Homicide. Mike walked into the large open room, which had eight industrial steel desks, all equipped with telephones and computers. The homicide unit was comprised of only five detectives, so three of the desks were left unoccupied to accommodate future expansion. The left side wall of the room was completely hidden by a tapestry of white boards, many of which were covered with names and notes written with erasable markers. Multicolored Post-it notes hung from each board, like the final leaves on an autumn tree. Along the opposite wall was a row of large gray file cabinets, thirty in all, packed with records from ongoing and unsolved investigations. A few tacky artificial plants, a brass coat rack, and an oil painting of a cowboy on a horse were the only attempts that were made at decorating. The room itself was dark and musty—the result of numerous burned out fluorescent bulbs and an inadequate heating and cooling system.

Mike stopped to exchange pleasantries with two of his detectives, Jeff Green and Steve Kraus, on his way toward his office, which was located just off the right rear corner of the room. Two other detectives, Dave Starbuck and Sandra Lara, were on the phones, but still acknowledged Mike's arrival with a couple of head gestures. Bob Stewart was the only detective who was missing due to an early morning meeting with a witness in one of his cases.

When he finally reached his office, Mike Groman was immediately startled by Floyd LeRud and Ray Schrader. They had arrived half an hour earlier at 7:30 AM, not wanting to be late on their first day.

"Good morning, Captain," said Floyd, who was immediately echoed by Ray. "Some storm!" he continued.

"Colder and wetter than a well digger's ass," Mike quipped.

Without missing a beat, Floyd asked, "So, Captain, how did you know that the victim was Nick Trikilos?"

"Easy, guys," Mike responded, "I just walked in the door. First, let me take you around so you can meet the rest of the team."

With that, Mike took Floyd and Ray from his office and made formal introductions to the four detectives who were present. They each seemed genuinely happy to meet the newcomers.

Without moving, Mike gave his standard tour of room 144 to Floyd and Ray. "Over there is the coffeemaker," he said, while pointing to the corner of the room and opposite his office. "And down the hall is a lounge with a refrigerator and a couple of vending machines. You can grab those desks over there—no one uses them. Make yourselves comfortable."

Captain Groman then dismissed himself saying, "Give me a few minutes, guys. I need to make a few phone calls and take care of some administrative bullshit."

With that, he walked back into his office and closed the door behind him.

CHAPTER ELEVEN

IT WOULD TAKE Captain Mike Groman about forty-five minutes to tend to his administrative duties. Floyd LeRud and Ray Schrader used that time agonizingly, taking inventory of the contents of their two desks. Between them, they had eight sharpened pencils of varying lengths, a stapler, two pairs of scissors, a ruler, a box of paper clips, seventeen multicolored rubber bands, a two-year-old calendar from State Farm Insurance, and a crusty and slightly cracked coffee mug from the Mount Lemmon Cafe.

Mike finally emerged from his office and ended their excruciating task by saying, "Ray, Floyd, come on in."

Once the two had taken their seats in the well-worn but still amply cushioned chairs that sat facing his desk, Mike apologetically said, "Sorry that took so long. Can I get you guys coffee?"

With that, Mike glanced over at a small table next to his desk where sat his own coffeemaker, a half dozen cleaned overturned cups, a container of artificial creamer, individual packets of sugar and sugar substitutes, and a number of plastic spoons.

Floyd graciously accepted the offer on behalf of both officers. "That would be great. Black, please."

Without getting up, Mike rolled his chair over to the small table and played host. It was clear to Floyd and Ray that he had repeated this maneuver many times.

"I take it that you guys are itching to know about Nick Trikilos."

Floyd and Ray were surprised that Captain Groman was able to sense their overwhelming curiosity.

"Well," Mike began as he opened up two file folders on his desk, "to understand how our dear friend Nick ended up dead with a golf club sticking out of his head requires a little bit of a history lesson, so bear with me guys."

Nick "the Trick" Trikilos was born on January 21, 1948, in Brooklyn, New York. His father, mother, and brother emigrated from Greece in 1945 shortly after the end of World War II. Nick was the middle child, flanked on either side by his older brother and younger sister.

Although very bright and articulate, Nick dropped out of school in the eighth grade, preferring to run the streets and pursue the lifestyle of a hoodlum. His best friend growing up was an Italian kid named Johnny Battaglia. Johnny's father, known as Batts to everyone in the neighborhood, owned a barbershop, which served as a convenient front for his primary enterprise of gambling. While the boys were in grade school, Batts paid Johnny and Nick a dollar a week to clean the shop after it had closed. It was good money at that time for a couple of kids. As the boys got older, Batts gave them more duties, none of which involved cleaning.

Batts Battaglia had grown up in Brooklyn as well and was a good childhood friend of Joseph "Bananas" Bonnano, who, by this time, had become a very powerful, influential, and infamous person in New York City. He was the founder of one of the five major crime families that made up the mafia or La Cosa Nostra, along with the Genovese, Lucchese, Gambino, and Columbo families. These five families were responsible for the lion's share of racketeering, loan-sharking, murder, pornography, gambling, conspiracy, money laundering, and drug trafficking. Their criminal enterprises had captured the imagination of the country and would serve as fodder for big-budget motion pictures for decades to come.

Every Tuesday, Joseph Bonnano would stop and see his friend Batts for a haircut and shave. He never paid, and he never had to wait.

Bonnano believed that the strength and success of La Cosa Nostra hinged on blood relations and shared traditional and strict Sicilian values. Although the inner circle of his criminal enterprise was limited to only these blood relations, friends like Batts could become what the family called "associates." It was in this environment that Nick Trikilos spent his formative years.

Though the five crime families were allies, they faced competition from rival organizations and often their clashes were quite bloody. Although never proven, it was rumored that in 1965, Batts arranged for a then-seventeen-year-old Nick Trikilos to hit a member of a rival family that had somehow crossed the Bonannos. Nick perceived this hit as justice and was more than willing and eager to prove himself to the Bonnano organization. In an emotionless and calculated execution, Nick supposedly walked up behind his target in a crowded bar, placed a .38 caliber revolver to the base of his victim's skull and without hesitation pulled the trigger, spraying the victim's blood over thirty or so patrons. During the ensuing chaos, Nick dropped the weapon and calmly walked out the front door. The customers, traumatized by the event, were unable to assist the police in making a positive identification of the shooter.

Shortly thereafter, Nick Trikilos moved to Mt. Holly, New Jersey, presumably to let things cool down. He would never return to Brooklyn. In an unrelated criminal investigation years later, it was revealed that Batts Battaglia wired Nick money every month for the next two years, although the police were never able to make the connection between the payments and the hit. It was there in Mt. Holly, with no marketable skills that Nick picked up the game of golf. He joined the posh Wedgewood Country Club and as it was told, used to pay the club house attendants a dollar to start his car. He claimed the reason for this was that he did not like getting into a hot car in the summer or a cold one in the winter. The fact of the matter was, however, that he was afraid of a bomb.

In 1960, John F. Kennedy was elected the thirty-fifth president of the United States. After taking the oath of office on a cold January morning in 1961, he began the task of forming his administration. He appointed his younger brother Robert F. Kennedy, a successful lawyer, to be the head of the Justice Department—the United States Attorney General.

Robert Kennedy targeted organized crime and attacked it like a heat-seeking missile, using the entire resources of the United States government. By 1965, the mafia, while not completely eliminated, was severely crippled. Robert Kennedy parlayed his notoriety from this work into a successful campaign for United States senator for the state of New York in 1966. Other prosecutors with political ambitions used his template for success and continued the attack on organized crime at both the state and local levels. The glory days of the Mafia would soon come to an end.

In 1968, Robert F. Kennedy, in an attempt to continue his slain brother's work, ran for president of the United States. On June 5, while campaigning in California, he was gunned down like his brother before him, leaving many conspiracy theorists believing that their assassinations were payback from organized crime.

In 1969, Joseph Bonnano retired and moved his family to Tucson, Arizona. The heads of the other crime families likewise opted to spend their post-mafia days in warm climates and resettled in parts of Florida, California, Nevada, and of course, Arizona. The five families of the La Cosa Nostra have weakly survived to the present day and are still run by blood relatives of the original family members.

Nick's older brother, Andreas, followed a different career path. He was an honor student at Brooklyn's' Roosevelt High School and earned a merit scholarship to Columbia University. Andreas graduated with a degree in political science and decided to pursue a career in law. Shortly after graduation, he applied to a number of law schools and chose to attend the University of Arizona in Tucson. He graduated in 1969, passed the Arizona bar exam, and was immediately hired by the law firm of Callesen, Michel & Robb.

Nick decided to move to Arizona in 1969 for two reasons. First, although he had little in common with his brother's law-abiding lifestyle, he was always very close to Andreas and felt comfortable staying with him until he got on his feet. Second, he knew the Bonnanos personally from his days in the barbershop and thought that if they were going to set up shop in Arizona, they might need a loyal soldier, even a Greek.

When Nick arrived in Tucson on that typical sweltering mid-July day, he was unaware that this move was going to change his life dramatically. He settled in with his brother who had just purchased a beautiful house in an upscale part of town, which was known to all the locals simply as Sabino Canyon. This area is named after a popular tourist destination and is the only place in Tucson where water flows naturally all year long. As chance would have it, Andreas's next-door neighbor had just sold his home to a Hollywood actress who was looking for a desert retreat. Tucson's close proximity to Los Angeles and the home's secluded location offered the starlet privacy and a place to unwind, yet still enabled her to return to work at a moments notice.

Erin Kelly was considered by many to be the most glamorous and sexiest actress at that time. On one of her stays, she somehow befriended her new neighbor Nick Trikilos. Though definitely not interested in him romantically, Erin became fast friends with Nick and the two spent hours together. One day out by the pool at Erin's house, Nick was conveniently experimenting with a new camera and decided to familiarize himself with its features and capabilities while taking pictures of Erin, who playfully obliged by posing as sexually as she could while not exposing herself. One of the pictures, after being developed, was incredible. The sun highlighted Erin's flowing blonde hair, gorgeous face, and shapely body in a captivating way.

Upon seeing the picture, the little wheels in Nick's Greek head began spinning. He approached Erin with a business proposition. He wanted to enlarge the picture, make copies and sell them in stores. In return, he would give Erin $1.00 for every picture of her that sold. Erin thought this was somewhat of a dumb idea, but agreed so as to avoid insulting her friend. To make it all legal, Andreas drew up a simple contract.

By 1971, the poster of Erin Kelly, emerging from her swimming pool, ended up on hundreds of thousands of bedroom walls around the country. This poster was the first of its kind and paved the way for today's athletes, musicians, supermodels, movie stars, and many others to grace our walls with their images.

Nick Trikilos became a very wealthy man at the ripe old age of twenty-four. He would spend the next thirty-six years dabbling in a variety of

business ventures with a modicum of success, but thanks to his poster idea, never really had to work another day in his life.

With the completion of the Nick Trikilos biography and the brief history lesson, Mike Groman began telling the story of his involvement.

"When the Bonnano family retired to Tucson in 1969, the Justice Department sent the Tucson Police copies of their files. We were supposed to keep and eye on them. We didn't want those goddamn gangsters turning Tucson into another Brooklyn. Their records indicated that about fifteen or so of Bonnano's henchmen, both major and minor players, had also moved here with Joseph Bonnano."

Pausing, Mike continued, "Because they all had felony convictions, we were able to roust them periodically, just to let them know we were watching."

"When I joined the force, my first partner was a tough old son of a bitch by the name of Frank Nausin. He retired four years later. He had been given the name of Nick Trikilos to check on."

After taking a sip of his now cold coffee, Mike continued, "Nick had a felony conviction back in 1966 for assault, and his name appeared in the file listing him as a minor player in the Bonnano organization. Before I arrived, my partner paid him a visit every few months. By the time I joined the force in 1976, those visits had almost stopped. It was obvious that the Bonnano retirement meant exactly that. I did meet Nick Trikilos a few times, and I was always fascinated with the story of his deal with Erin Kelly. I had her poster hanging on a wall in my dorm at college. Boy, she had a great set."

Mike concluded his talk with Floyd and Ray on a somewhat sentimental note. "The last time I saw Nick Trikilos was back in 1985," and then added, "until yesterday. He definitely looked older, but you'd never forget the face."

By now, the coffee had made its way through Floyd LeRud, Ray Schrader, and Mike Groman. They all agreed it was time for a quick break and they would meet again in ten minutes.

When Mike was out of earshot, Floyd turned to Ray and asked incredulously, "What in the hell did we just step in?"

CHAPTER TWELVE

THE THREE RECONVENED in Captain Groman's office a short time later. Mike continued his earlier conversation with Floyd and Ray by saying, "I don't want the two of you reading too much into the organized crime angle. There hasn't been any indication of Nick Trikilos's involvement in any of that shit for over forty years." Mike's language was often salty, although his use of profanity was normally limited to the company of his detectives. His wife was very active in their church, and vulgarities were not permitted in the Groman home.

Mike tried to offer a plausible alternative motive. "Nick was also a businessman, so he probably pissed off a number of people over the years. No matter what, you can bet we will follow the trail of evidence wherever it leads."

It was now 10:30 AM and time for Mike, Floyd, and Ray to get to work.

Mike turned to Ray Schrader to give him his first assignment. "Go to the Department of Motor Vehicles computer link and pull up the photo of Nick Trikilos, enlarge it, and make about a dozen copies. Take one over to the golf course and show it to those four employees—Sandy, Pete, Don, and, um, who am I missing?"

"Donna," Ray replied. "She's the manager of the Bar."

"That's right, Donna. She's a real piece of work. Pay particular attention to what she has to say. Other than the killer, she was probably the last one to see Nick alive. See if any of them can remember something about Nick, who he was with, what he did, anything at all. Then, help them finish up their work on those lists of people who were at the golf course on Tuesday. As soon as you're finished, head on back."

Mike was keenly aware that he had a tendency to micromanage and immediately felt embarrassed that he had stated the obvious. Mike thought to himself, *Where in the hell else would he go, Disneyland?* Ray apparently did not notice so Mike let the subject drop.

Without hesitation and with a rush of adrenaline, Ray exited Captain Groman's office to eagerly tackle his first solo assignment as a homicide detective.

One of Mike's strengths as captain was his ability to maximize the use of his human resources. Knowing that Ray was the least experienced of the two, Mike gave him an assignment that was simple in nature and required very little actual detective work. By contrast, he chose to spend the day with Floyd, as the two would search for clues at the victim's home and conduct what Mike knew would be a difficult interview with Nick's brother.

Now alone with Floyd LeRud, Mike outlined their plan for the day. "Grab your coat. We're going to head over to Nick's place to see if we can find anything." After a short pause, he added, "Then we have a two o'clock appointment with his brother at his law office. We'll see what he knows."

Captain Groman normally spent his days stuck behind his desk, shuffling bureaucratic papers and giving his detectives help and guidance. He relished these occasional opportunities that allowed him to get back to his investigatory roots. Mike had been an exceptional field detective and accepted his promotion to the head of the homicide unit with mixed emotions. The determining factor in his decision ultimately came down to his increasing physical limitations.

Just as Mike and Floyd were preparing to depart the office, Detective Sandra Lara, with the telephone pressed against her chest to muffle her voice, said, "Captain, I've got a guy on the line . . . he says he played golf with Nick Trikilos the day he was murdered."

Mike replied, "I'll take it in my office."

Mike gave Floyd a signal to wait for him outside as he rushed back to pick up his phone.

"This is Captain Groman, how can I help you?"

Mike listened for a few moments, and after offering a brief condolence asked, "Where can we meet?" After another short pause, Mike ended the call by saying, "We'll be there in twenty minutes."

After hanging up the phone, Mike reemerged from his office and said to a puzzled Floyd LeRud, "Change of plans."

CHAPTER THIRTEEN

TUCSON, ARIZONA, ONLY receives about twelve inches of rain each year. The summer monsoon accounts for half of that amount while the winter rain makes up the remainder. During the summer, subtropical moisture combines with the intense desert heat resulting in daily hit-and-miss thunderstorms, many of which can be quite severe. The winter rain arrives in more of a traditional manner, with cold fronts from the west passing through southern Arizona about once a week.

The current weather system was born in the Gulf of Alaska, so when the storm hit Tucson, it delivered a particularly cold Arctic blast. While not a very wet storm, the snow level had dropped to about 3,500 feet, which was low enough in altitude to give the residents living in the foothills of Tucson's surrounding mountains an unusual light dusting of snow.

Although it had just stopped raining, the moisture on the road was kicked up by the cars in front of Mike and Floyd, which required them to use the intermittent setting on the windshield wipers.

The mystery caller with whom Mike had briefly chatted before abruptly leaving the station was Steve Brennan, who lived on the far east side of town. Because the station was located on the opposite end of the city, the two had agreed to meet at an approximate halfway point at Jerry-Bobs Restaurant on Speedway Boulevard. The small but quaint mom-and-pop establishment was popular for breakfast, although their lunches and dinners left something to be desired.

It was almost 11:00 AM when Mike and Floyd arrived. Jerry-Bobs was almost empty, as the breakfast crowd had already left, while the customers for lunch would not arrive for close to another hour.

With only two single patrons seated in the restaurant, Mike took the initiative and approached the closest, who was seated at a booth. "Are you Steve?"

Steve stood up, shook hands with the two detectives, and warmly said, "Yes, hi! I'm Steve Brennan."

The fifty-year-old ex-marine, who still looked fit, was wearing a white cotton shirt, khaki pants, and a brown bombardier jacket. His short thinning brown hair was curly, and though he was of European decent, he probably had a fantastic afro back in the day. His skin's slightly orange hue indicated that his tan had been acquired in a salon, rather than on a beach. His only jewelry was a simple wedding band and a very expensive watch.

After the introductions, the three sat down and ordered coffee.

"I'm so sorry about your friend Nick," Mike began.

Steve replied eulogistically, "He was a heck of a nice guy and a good friend for almost ten years."

After a short pause, Mike pulled out his notebook and asked, "Do you mind if I jot down a few things while we talk?"

"Not at all."

"Can I ask how the two of you met?"

"Nick's brother Andreas and I served on the board of directors for Casa de los Niños, which as the two of you probably know is a charitable organization that provides all sorts of services to abused children. I met Nick at a fundraiser, and we hit it off. He is," Steve said, and then paused to correct himself, "he *was* a heck of a golfer. We played together almost every Tuesday. He was a lot of fun."

"What kind of work do you do, Steve?"

"I'm the owner and general manager of Fitz."

"I'm sorry, what is Fitz?"

"You're obviously not an eastsider," answered Steve.

"That's right," Mike said. "I live up near Ina and La Canada and don't get to your part of town very often." Actually, Mike's home and Fitz were on the complete opposite ends of the city limits.

"Fitz is a fitness center and racquet club," explained Steve. "We also have a banquet facility and offer a full catering service."

Although Mike was unfamiliar with Fitz, Floyd had actually considered joining the club, which was the closest workout facility to where he lived, but he could not afford the dues. Floyd, however, realized that his role in this questioning was to keep quiet, so he did not pipe in to offer this information.

Mike jotted down a few notes and then cut to the chase. "Can you tell me about the last time you saw Nick?"

"We played golf on Tuesday like always," said Steve. "We had a tee time at 11:00 because Nick insisted on waiting until it warmed up a little. We played the Dell Urich course at the Randolph Golf Complex."

"Who else rounded out your foursome?"

"I knew you would ask," said Steve as he handed Captain Groman the scorecard from that round of golf.

The scorecard had four names written on it: Nick, Steve, Tony and Mark. Nick shot a 77, Steve and Tony each shot an 83, while Mark finished with a 91.

"I'm not much of a golfer," said Mike, "but Nick's 77 is pretty impressive."

"For Nick, a 77 was not a particularly good round. He was a two handicapper," Steve responded. "On that course, he usually shot a 72 or 73."

Having finished their discussion of Nick Trikilos's golfing prowess, Mike continued, "Can you tell me anything about Tony and Mark?"

"They didn't appear to know each other, and you know, I didn't think to ask. They were probably a couple of walk-ons that just wound up in our game. They seemed like good guys—we had a lot of laughs. Some golfers take the game too seriously—do you know what I mean?"

"I sure do," answered Mike. "I played last summer with a guy who got pissed off with every bad shot, and believe me, he had a lot of them. He was throwing clubs and acting like a jackass. None of us had any fun."

Mike then changed the subject by asking, "What did you do when you finished playing?"

"The four of us went into the Bar and had a couple of pitchers of beer. Then I had to take off. The wife and I were going out to dinner and a movie."

"What time was that?"

"About 4:30."

Then, in what was an obvious attempt to check Steve's alibi, Mike asked, "So where did you eat and what movie did you see?"

"I knew you would also be asking me that. Here is our ticket stub from the Cineplex," Steve said proudly as he handed Mike his stub for the 7:00 PM showing of *No Country for Old Men* and then digging for his wallet, continued, "let me find our credit card receipt from Francesca's where we ate dinner."

Satisfied, Mike continued the questioning, "So, when you left Nick at the Bar, was he still with Tony and Mark?"

"Yeah, I left the three of them together. They had just ordered another pitcher."

Steve then gave Mike a brief description of his golfing partners and finished up by handing Mike his business card.

"That's about it," said Mike. "Thanks for all of your help. We'll be in touch if there is anything else."

"Anything I can do," Steve responded.

Mike picked up the check, and after shaking hands, the three left Jerry-Bobs. Steve drove away in his 2007 Chevy Tahoe back in the direction of Fitz, while Mike and Floyd headed in the opposite direction toward Nick's place.

Floyd was very quiet throughout the interview, but as they drove, he finally had a chance to comment. "Wow, that guy was helpful—maybe a little too helpful. Who keeps their movie stubs? He seemed a little too quick to produce an alibi."

Mike attempted to calm the overly suspicious rookie. "I don't think that Steve is the murderer. There needs to be a motive. Those two were friends—if they were in some kind of a pissing contest, they probably wouldn't be playing golf together."

After Mike had a couple of moments to consider Floyd's observations, and not wanting to sound dismissive, he added, "Other than the golf course employees, this is the first person we have spoken with. We need to gather a lot of facts before we can start zeroing in on a suspect."

Floyd knew that what Mike had said made sense. He couldn't help, however, be suspicious of Steve Brennan—something just didn't feel right.

CHAPTER FOURTEEN

THE RANDOLPH GOLF Complex was sparsely populated Thursday morning, although there were a few diehard golfers who had donned rain gear and braved the cold winter storm that had lingered for the better part of two days. The sky would begin to clear later in the morning and more golfers would arrive, but it would be a generally slow day.

The Bar was closed, of course, and there were signs posted on both the north and south entrances that read:

CLOSED
SORRY FOR THE
INCONVIENIENCE

These were the same signs regularly used by the custodial staff when they closed the restrooms for ten minutes to clean. Now these signs would grace the two entrances to the Bar indefinitely. Outside, tables and chairs from the Bar were neatly stacked under the covered patio, while inside a crew from Floor World removed the gray, tattered, and now blood-stained carpet in small, manageable sections. Earlier, other workers had secured the premises by bolting pieces of plywood over the shattered southern door until a glazer could be summoned to replace the glass. The scattered glass fragments outside the door had been cleaned up and removed the day before by the TCSU, and the lab technicians were currently in the process of painstakingly examining each piece in search of evidence.

Sandy, Pete, Don, and Donna were all jammed inside Pete's crowded office. To provide an area where the four could work together, Pete had moved a number of large boxes from his office out into the hallway and commandeered three old folding chairs from the broom closet so that the four could work together in the same area.

When Officer Ray Schrader arrived, the four were feverishly pouring over credit card receipts, employee work records, and the computerized lists of the tee time reservations.

"How's it going?" Ray asked casually, as he stood in the hallway next to a case of golf balls. The office was so crowded that he was only able to peek his head inside. Before they could respond, he asked, "Anything I can do to help?"

Pete recognized Officer Schrader, even though he was not in uniform. "I think we've got a good handle on it. We're done with everything except the credit card receipts. We are putting them in order by when the purchases were made."

Ray had expected just a stack of receipts but appreciated the chronological organization. "Wow, that's great!"

While the four continued their task, Sandy, without looking up, asked, "Did you find his car?"

Ray was caught off guard, as he was accustomed to asking, but not answering questions. "Who's car?" he asked.

"The dead guy's car. Unless someone drove him here, it should have been in the parking lot Wednesday morning. The lot was empty when I arrived." Sandy then repeated her question, "So where's his car?"

Not wanting to look incompetent, Ray answered, "We're working on it."

Pete sensed from Ray's hesitancy and confusion at Sandy's question that the car had not yet been located. He suggested, "You might want to try the auxiliary lot just to the north of here by the tennis complex.

Tuesday was very busy, and he may have parked next door. It happens all the time."

Not wanting to look foolish, Ray excused himself by saying, "It looks like you folks have a handle on everything here. I think I'll go out and poke around a bit and look for evidence that the CSU might have missed."

"No hurry," said Pete, "we've got at least another hour of work ahead of us."

After Ray had left the pro shop, Pete turned to Sandy and said, "He's going out to look for the car."

Sandy simply replied, "Yep!" With that, Pete, Sandy, Don, and Donna simultaneously broke into laughter.

Ray went directly to his patrol car and using his on-board computer, pulled up the license and registration of the vehicle belonging to Nick Trikilos. He then took a short walk to the auxiliary lot where he almost immediately discovered the white 2007 Cadillac Escalade, with the personalized license plate that read NIKTRIK.

When Ray returned to Pete's cramped office, Sandy looked up and smugly asked, "So, did you find it?"

Knowing that he had not fooled anyone, Ray came clean and gave credit where credit was due. "It was right next door where you said it would be."

A short time later, Don handed Officer Schrader the group's organized stack of papers. "Here's everything we've got."

After thanking them for their diligent work, Ray said, "I've got just one more thing I need you to help me with." Ray continued, not pausing long enough to allow for any objections. "I would like you to look at this photo and see if you can remember anything."

Ray showed the enlarged driver's license photo of Nick Trikilos to the four golf course employees. Sandy recalled immediately the bloody scene from the day before in what seemed to be a nightmarish flashback. Pete and Don acknowledged that the person in the photo looked somewhat familiar and guessed that perhaps he was one of their infrequent regulars who would play once or twice a month and had done so for quite some time. They also indicated that there was nothing special about him and that a lot of golfers fell into the same category.

Looking at his picture, without all of the blood and the protruding golf club, Sandy was able to recall periodically selling Nick Gatorade and that he was a good tipper. She finished by saying, "He was always just beginning his round of golf, and I was gone for the day by the time he was done."

Donna was much more helpful. "Oh, yeah, I know this guy. He comes in a few times a month, always with the same good-looking guy. They usually have too much to drink. The guy in the photo used to smoke some nasty cigars before the city banned smoking in public places a few years back."

"Do you remember seeing him on Tuesday?" Ray asked.

"Yeah, he was in here that day. There were four of them who sat in the back corner by the TV."

"Four of them?" Ray interrupted.

"Yeah. The four of them—the guy in the picture, his good-looking friend, and the two other guys that I didn't recognize."

"Can you describe his good-looking friend?"

"Tall, well built, tan, short curly brown hair . . . never seemed interested," Donna answered, indicating that her repeated attempts at seduction had failed.

Ray didn't bother asking her if she would recognize him again. "How about the other two?"

"I didn't pay much attention to them. I don't think I've seen them before." Donna paused, as if searching her brain for any recollection of the other two men. "The one guy was kind of heavy with a round face and dark hair. I don't remember the other one at all."

"How do you remember there were four of them?"

"I gave them two pitchers of beer and four glasses. They all helped carry them back to their table. Miller MGD."

"Do you remember what time they came in and when they left?"

"I'm guessing they came in around 3:30. The good-looking guy and the one I can't remember left together at about 4:30. I noticed because our food delivery service guy always comes at the same time each day. The good-looking guy held the door for him. The dead guy and the round-faced guy stayed until closing at 7:00. They were the last ones in the Bar.

I assumed the round-faced guy was driving because the dead guy was shit faced. He started drinking bourbon after the pitchers of beer."

Ray thought for a moment and asked, "What door did they go out?"

"I don't know," Donna answered. "I didn't actually see them leave. I went back to the kitchen and was putting stuff away. When I came back out, they were gone." Then, as if a light bulb had just turned on, Donna realized that her oversight may have resulted in a dead guy ending up on the floor of the Bar. "I just assumed they'd left. They must have been back in the locker room. Like I told you and your partner yesterday," Donna continued as she changed her previous testimony ever so slightly, "after I *thought* everyone had left, I turned off the lights, locked the door and took off."

Ray finished their meeting by thanking Sandy, Pete, Don, and Donna for all of their help. As he carefully shuffled out of the cramped office, Ray turned to Donna and asked, "Do you think you would recognize Round Face again if you saw him?"

Donna answered hesitantly, "I think so."

CHAPTER FIFTEEN

THE LA PALOMA Country Club, located in the foothills of the Catalina Mountain Range that runs along Tucson's northern border, boasts a membership of the who's who of the city's social elite. The golf course is lined with multimillion-dollar homes, and residents are required to pay an association fee greater than many Tucsonan's mortgages or rent. The typical domicile consists of a single breadwinner, usually the husband, a wife who spends her days at the club, the junior league, or the mall, and the quintessential 2.5 children who attend the most expensive preparatory schools in southern Arizona, if not the entire southwest.

The Village at La Paloma is comprised of eighty-four attractive terra-cotta-colored luxury condominiums that sit adjacent to the La Paloma Country Club. These units were constructed in 1995, when the high rollers who lived in the lavish homes surrounding the La Paloma Country Club surprisingly lost a rezoning fight that allowed for the construction of high-density housing on their doorsteps. While still relatively pricey, the condominium complex was considered blight by some of the foothill's snootier residents.

Nick Trikilos purchased unit 63 in 2002. After losing his third house in as many divorce settlements, he joked that he was trying to change his luck by trying something different. The fact of the matter was that he had become wary of homeownership and preferred the more carefree lifestyle of a low-maintenance condominium.

Cheryl Polley was the manager of the Village and had read of Nick Trikilos's death in the morning paper, the *Arizona Daily Star*. As a result, this forty-two-year-old brunette with an engaging smile was not surprised when two homicide detectives walked into her office shortly after noon. Following the formal introductions, Floyd took out a small notepad in anticipation of the questioning that would ensue, and Mike did not disappoint. "Ms. Polley, how long had you known Mr. Trikilos?"

Thinking for a moment, she answered, "About five or six years. I was working here when he first moved in."

"How well did you know him?"

"Well, I probably only talked to him maybe once a year. Every January, he threw himself his own birthday bash in our recreation center. He always came in around Thanksgiving to make the reservation."

"Were there ever any problems with Mr. Trikilos?"

"Like what?" Ms. Polley asked.

Mike quickly rattled off a series of questions. "Did he have any run-ins with the neighbors? Were there any complaints about too much noise or late night parties? Were the police ever called to his unit? Anything like that?"

"Oh, heavens no. He was a model resident. I wish I could say the same for everyone here. We have a large number of younger residents, and some of their parties have gotten out of control."

After some thought, Cheryl added, "Oh, wait a second—I can think of one thing. About two years ago we had a small situation, but it was really no big deal."

"What was that?" Mike asked.

"Well, someone inside Mr. Trikilos's unit broke out his window with a wine bottle. Glass was scattered all over a common walkway. He had it replaced the very next day and cleaned up the glass himself."

"Did he ever say who did it?"

"I saw him the next day when he was picking up his mail. All he said was that his girlfriend had too much to drink, and they got into a silly fight."

"You wouldn't happen to know her name?" asked Mike.

There were a few things that Captain Groman was certain of at this point in the investigation. First, there was no way that Cheryl Polley would know the name of Nick's girlfriend. He asked more or less as a courtesy to the manager and wanted her to feel that she was being helpful. He also knew that Nick Trikilos's death did not come at the hands of a woman—too violent, too gory. Then, his chauvinistic tendencies that his wife had almost completely extricated from his personality surfaced, as he mused to himself, "A woman would never kill with a golf club—maybe a vacuum cleaner or an iron, but never a golf club." He was immediately ashamed of himself.

Cheryl Polley explained that she wouldn't know any of Nick Trikilos's visitors. She respected the privacy of the residents in the Village and had kept her personal contact with each both professional and brief. She added, however, "I know that his brother and his family came to visit on numerous occasions. I don't know his name, but the family resemblance was obvious. His brother was just a larger version of Mr. Trikilos."

"Is there anything else you can add?" Mike finished, having run out of questions for the condominium manager.

"Not really," she said, "except that he always left the recreation center spotless after he used it. Most people just leave it a mess."

"Oh my!" she added as Mike and Floyd began gathering their belonging to leave, "his birthday is next week, or I mean, would have been next week," she said as her voice trailed off.

On that somber note, Floyd asked for the key to unit 63 and directions to the condo of Nick Trikilos.

The short walkway leading up to Nick's unit was tastefully landscaped on either side with desert vegetation. Under the covered entryway were two large colorful ceramic Mexican pots, which each contained fox-tailed ferns.

Once inside, both detectives were shocked at what they saw. "I have never in my life seen a bachelor's place look like this," Floyd said with amazement.

"Just look at this fucking place," Mike chimed in, echoing Floyd's sentiment.

The living area was stunning and immaculate. The furnishings were not only high end, but top of the line. Muted earth tones set the overall mood, while an array of brightly colored accent pieces brought the place to life. A number of De Grazia originals, along with an expensive Navajo rug, tied the handcrafted southwestern furniture together into a Santa Fe style showplace. The centerpiece of the room, however, was an original Fritz Scholder painting that rounded out his Native American imagery. This he got from the estate of a Phoenix collector, who died unexpectedly and whose lawyer owed Nick quite a lot of money. The inheritors lived out of state, and there was no record of the painting or its value.

In the kitchen, the granite countertop was uncluttered, holding only three stainless steel canisters of varying sizes and an espresso machine that probably had never been used. The Sub-Zero refrigerator and freezer matched the stove and dishwasher, also with a stainless steel finish. The somewhat antiseptic and industrial appearance of the kitchen was softened by the custom cabinetry, which was also of a southwestern design.

Nick's unit was a two-bedroom model, one of which was converted into an office. The tasteful décor of the living area permeated these other rooms as well, and they demonstrated his eclectic tastes.

The master suite had taken on an oriental theme as teak now dominated the room. The walls were adorned with numerous oil paintings that he had picked up on a trip to Japan just a few years earlier. A number of small, handcrafted jade sculptures were arranged strategically on both the dresser and chest of drawers, drawing one's eye away from the brightly colored Asian paintings. The walk-in closet held Nick's entire wardrobe, which was quite extensive. Each article of clothing was precisely positioned on hangers and stood like soldiers at attention.

The second bedroom was converted into an office and was more functional than esthetically pleasing. A highly polished large mesquite desk housed the latest in technological gadgetry, while a large file cabinet was tucked in the closet and out of view. The only decorations in the room were two Ansel Adams prints that were positioned on the largest wall and a number of family photos arranged in three small clusters.

While Mike began rummaging through the large file cabinet in the closet, Floyd began exploring the contents of the desk. There, in the top drawer, he discovered Nick's day planner, which in a homicide investigation can be a mother lode of information. A skillful investigator can use it as a roadmap to piece together the victim's life leading up to the moment of death. In some cases, the final entry would actually name the killer.

The condition of the entire condominium indicated the occupant paid an acute attention to detail, and Nick Trikilos's day planner was no different. Though the entries were cryptic, his days were outlined by the hour, sometimes by the minute. It appeared that in some cases Nick may have spent more time recording the activity in his day planner than actually doing the deed.

Floyd shared with Mike the discovery of Nick's day planner, which proved to be the highlight of their search of the victim's home. Nick's file cabinet was surprisingly empty, containing warranty information on his household appliances, car maintenance receipts, and a few folders with various legal documents primarily from his three divorce decrees. As a result, the two detectives left the condominium somewhat disappointed. Mike did arrange for the TCSU to pick up Nick's computer, hoping that their search through its hard drive might yield some results.

The drive from Nick's to Andreas Trikilos's downtown office would take about a half an hour. The roads were now dry, and the sun was fighting desperately to break through the remaining dark clouds. As Floyd drove, Mike poured through Nick's fifteen-month day planner, trying to make sense of its complicated code.

CHAPTER SIXTEEN

MIKE AND FLOYD arrived at 110 North Stone Avenue about fifteen minutes prior to their scheduled meeting with Andreas Trikilos. His office was located on the ninth floor of a twenty-story glass-and-steel building. The name of the law firm on the mahogany door had expanded over the years from Callesen, Michael & Robb to Callesen, Michael, Robb, Bell, Sturgeon & Trikilos. Adding any more partners in the future would require smaller lettering or a larger door.

After a brief wait in the reception area, Mike and Floyd were escorted to Andreas Trikilos's office by his legal assistant.

He and Nick shared a strong family resemblance, although Andreas favored his rather large father while Nick was more like his diminutive mother. Facially, the two would always be paired as brothers.

Andreas Trikilos was a striking figure, impeccably dressed and well-groomed. His tie and shoes were Italian, while his dark gray suit with a light blue pinstripe did not come off the rack. A custom-fit plain white silk shirt and the obligatory Rolex watch completed the ensemble. His salt-and-pepper hair was quaffed to perfection—the result of his weekly appointment at Gadabout, a posh salon and day spa that catered to both men and women. It was easy to picture Andreas standing in a courtroom and swaying a jury by how he looked rather than by what he said.

"May I get you gentlemen something to drink—coffee, water, juice, anything?" he asked while seating Mike and Floyd into two leather chairs that faced his large oak desk.

After declining a beverage and offering his sincere condolences, Mike got down to business. "Are you sure you are up to answering some questions?" he began.

Andreas answered, "This is really tough. Nick and I were very close. My wife has two sisters, but she always looked at Nick as an older brother. She is devastated. And my two young boys—they just lost their favorite uncle."

Andreas was a bachelor until he was forty-seven years old. Patty was twenty years younger than Andreas when the two married in 1993, and the couple waited three years before starting their family. Their oldest child was twelve-year-old Andre, who was followed by Nickolas who had just turned nine.

Mike assured Andreas by saying, "We'll try to keep this brief. First of all, do you know of anyone that had a grudge or some kind of beef with your brother that could have done something like this?"

"I can't imagine," answered Andreas. "Everyone really liked Nick." But after pausing for a moment, he recalled, "There was this one guy a number of years ago who tried to sue my brother. His case never had any merit and was thrown out before it even went to trial, but this guy swore that he would get even."

"What was that all about?" asked Mike.

"Well," Andreas Trikilos began, searching his mind for the details, "Nick was part of an investment group that had purchased some land in Oro Valley, just north of Tucson. He had persuaded an acquaintance to invest in this residential subdivision, though within a few months, I think everyone involved in the project lost most of their money. An environmental group had jumped in and was able to prove that this land was a Spotted Owl sanctuary, so all of that land was protected by the federal government because apparently that bird is an endangered species. The investors were only able to recoup pennies on the dollar by selling off the small portion of the land that was inhabitable. So, oh Jesus, what was that guy's name? Oh yeah, Larry Reep. He brought this suit against Nick for his losses, claiming that this entire deal was a scheme and nothing more than fraud."

"We'll check out this Larry Reep," said Mike. "Is that spelled R-E-A-P?"

"Um, two Es, I think. I have the file somewhere because I helped Nick defend the suit. I'll have my secretary dig it out for you before you leave," said Andreas.

"That would be great." Changing the subject, Mike asked, "When was the last time you saw your brother alive?"

"He came over last Sunday like always," Andreas answered. "After his divorce in 2002, he started joining me, Patty, and the boys for church. He was kind of lonely at the time and just began spending the day with us. We'd watch sports while Patty would make dinner. He usually left about 5:00 PM. He was always afraid of imposing."

"And this past Sunday?" Mike asked getting Andreas back on track.

"Like always, we went to church, and then we watched football, the wild card playoffs were on. Patty made a pot roast."

"Did anything seem out of the ordinary or different? Did Nick seem OK?"

Andreas thought for a moment, trying to recall the previous week's events. "Everything was normal. Nick was Nick."

"What do you mean by Nick was Nick?"

"Nick was smart, funny, talkative, upbeat, and loved rough housing with the boys. When they started, Patty always stopped it by saying, 'Take it outside.' Like I said, Nick was Nick."

"Did he have any problems, financial or otherwise?" Mike continued.

"Patty and I suspected that Nick maybe drank too much," answered Andreas. "We don't drink at all, so he never did in our house. We'd see him occasionally at some functions, and we could tell that he'd had too much."

"Like at the Casa de los Niños fundraisers?" Mike asked, indicating to Andreas that he had already done some legwork.

Looking surprised, Andreas answered, "So you must have talked with Steve Brennan already."

Without acknowledging in the affirmative or negative, Mike asked, "What can you tell me about Steve Brennan?"

"Steve and I were on the board of Casa about ten years ago," Andreas said. "He is a great guy. We put on four fundraisers each year, once a quarter. Nick and Steve met at one of them and became good friends. They have been playing golf together every Tuesday for years. They probably played this past Tuesday when—"

He stopped himself immediately and said to the inquisitive Mike Groman, "I can guarantee you that he had nothing to do with Nick's death," and then repeated, "Guarantee it!"

Mike then changed the subject back to Nick's finances, knowing that this can often be a motive. "With his divorce, and that Oro Valley deal that went bust, how was Nick doing financially?"

Andreas appreciated the different line of questioning. "Financially, Nick was just fine. He made a bundle about twenty-five years ago."

"On the Erin Kelly deal?" Mike interrupted.

Again surprised at Mike's knowledge, Andreas continued, "Yes, on the Erin Kelly deal. He used that money and made numerous investments over the years and most of them were very successful."

"You mentioned that Nick was divorced, did he take a financial hit on that?"

"He was actually divorced three times. His longest marriage lasted just under a year. His last wife was named Kathy. I really liked her. I thought that one would last."

"How did he come out in the settlements?"

"Because he had been married each time for such a short period, the amount he paid in alimony was inconsequential. He generously gave each of them the house, although they were purchased with a minimal down payment. He never had any kids."

Andreas told Mike and Floyd that he was the executor of Nick's will and estate and that he would be able to give a more accurate assessment of his finances, but it would take quite some time.

Without comment, Mike changed the subject once again. "What can you tell me about his relationship with Joseph Bonnano?"

This question immediately irritated Andreas. "Look, all that crap happened over forty years ago. Nick did some things he was not very proud of. He had a lot of regrets. I know he was involved in some bad shit, but I never asked him about it."

In an obvious attempt to focus the detectives' attention on Nick's positive contributions to society, Andreas asked, "Did you know that Nick volunteered a few hours twice a week assembling kitchen cabinets for Habitat for Humanity? Did you know that he also spent countless hours working for Casa de los Niños? The old Nick Trikilos and this Nick Trikilos are two different people."

Neither agreeing nor disagreeing, Mike again changed the subject by pulling out Nick's day planner. "Can you take a look through this and tell me if anything jumps out at you?"

Andreas asked, "Why would anything jump out at me? I mean, it's just a day planner."

Mike answered, "Well, maybe you could just take a look through it. The problem is that although his activity is very detailed, the planner is filled with initials and abbreviations, almost like a code."

Andreas said, "I've never seen it, but I know a good deal of what he did, and I might be able to translate."

With that, the three spent the next hour pouring over the day planner and were successful at deciphering a good number of the cryptic entries. Many of the initials belonged to Nick's business partners or associates whom Andreas was able to match with specific companies. A number of the other entries indicated restaurants—for example, HDS stood for the Hacienda del Sol Restaurant. Andreas explained that Nick never ate at home; in fact, his Sub-Zero refrigerator contained only water, juice, and beer, while the freezer only had ice. Dinners and lunches were usually both business and pleasure activities, many times lasting for hours. HFH frequently appeared in the afternoon blocks on Mondays and Thursdays, and as Andreas had indicated, stood for Habitat for Humanity. Golf courses also appeared in initials on Tuesdays. The final entry, DU for Dell Urich chillingly appeared on the date of Nick's death.

Mike couldn't help but ask, "Why do you think Nick wrote like that in his day planner?" somewhat expecting Andreas to reveal some sinister motive.

Andreas, almost chuckling, answered, "Nick was not a very modern guy, but a few years ago, he picked up text messaging, and for some reason, he thought all of the abbreviations were somehow cool."

A disappointed Mike Groman was still appreciative of the fact that he had at least been trained to decode Nick's day planner.

The time had flown by. It was now about a quarter of four when Mike apologized to Andreas Trikilos for taking up so much of his time. Andreas reassured Mike that it was not a problem.

As earlier promised, Andreas's secretary provided a copy of the file on the Larry Reep suit. "Can I keep this?" asked Mike.

"Those are just copies of all the paperwork. They're yours."

With that, Andreas Trikilos began escorting the two detectives from his office.

Halfway out, Mike stopped abruptly and asked, "What type of law do you practice?"

Andreas answered, "We're a full service firm—divorce, contracts, estate planning, criminal defense, real estate, personal injury—you name it."

"But what is your specialty?" Mike asked.

After a brief pause, Andreas Trikilos hesitantly answered, "I'm a criminal defense attorney."

CHAPTER SEVENTEEN

IT WAS SHORTLY after noon when Ray Schrader returned to the squad room from his meeting with Sandy, Pete, Don, and Donna at the Randolph Golf Complex. He would spend the remainder of that afternoon organizing and cataloging all of the tee times, reservations, and credit card receipts, while Mike Groman and Floyd LeRud met with Andreas Trikilos.

Golf courses send off golfers in groups of four, which (unsurprisingly) are referred to as "foursomes." Beginning at the crack of dawn, the first foursome is sent off by "the starter" for eighteen holes of fun or sometimes eighteen holes of frustration. The next seven to eight minutes, and every seven to eight minutes after that, another foursome is sent on its way. This system allows for the golfers to play at a comfortable pace so that they feel neither delayed nor rushed. At this time of the year, the first tee times at Randolph and Dell Urich were at 7:45 AM.

On the day Nick Trikilos was murdered, Ray learned from the golf course's records and receipts that there were a total of 120 tee times, 60 on each course, for a total of 480 golfers. Four hundred and sixteen paid with credit cards, eight used a rain check, and thirteen redeemed gift certificates, leaving forty-three who paid with cash. Of those forty-three, thirty-nine had reservations, and four did not. Although hopeful that the killer would be traceable through one of these records or receipts, Ray was fearful that he (or she) was one of the four who paid with cash, did not have a reservation, and left without a paper trail.

The records also indicated that Nick Trikilos and Steve Brennan booked an 11:07 tee time on Dell Urich a week in advance. They were joined by two single players, Mark Schenck and Lawson Bramblett, who made their reservations the previous Saturday and Sunday respectively. On Tuesday, the day the four played, Nick Trikilos and Steve Brennan each paid with their Visa cards, while Mark Schenck used his Discover card and Lawson Bramblett his American Express.

While Ray was working, the only other detective in the squad room was Mike Gorman's second in command, Dave Starbuck. "Dave, is it?" Ray asked, now needing some assistance and unsure of the officer's name, having just met all of the detectives in the squad earlier that day.

"That's right, Dave Starbuck," he answered as he looked up from a stack of papers. "Do you need some help?"

"Yeah, I've got a few credit card receipts from some suspects, and I need to find out their addresses and phone numbers. What do I do?"

"Wow, only a few hours on the job and already you've got some suspects. I'm impressed," said Dave in a subtly sarcastic and mocking tone.

Whether Dave's comment was ignored or just unnoticed, Ray, undeterred, went on to explain how he acquired the names and credit card receipts of the victim's playing partners—Steve Brennan, Mark Schenck, and Lawson Bramblett. Ray then said, "I also got a pretty good description of two of them from the waitresses in the Bar." Then, after a brief pause, he added, "I also want to run the names of the last few groups that played that day. I'm thinking that they may have been in the Bar and may have overheard or noticed some altercation involving Nick Trikilos when he was drunk."

Suddenly impressed, Dave took the newbie much more seriously and offered his help. "On the other end of the building, go to room 204. There are these two computer geeks, they've got some kind of title, and tell them what you need. They'll work their magic."

"How long will it take?" Ray asked.

"If they're not busy, a couple of minutes." Jokingly Dave added, "They can probably tell you what they had for breakfast this morning. They're amazing!"

Both Ray and Floyd had worked out of the East Side Substation, a small complex that was a far cry from the sprawling downtown headquarters where they were now assigned. The original part of the building was constructed in the early 1950s, but additions had been added on seven different occasions to accommodate the growth of the department. These additions rendered the headquarters a virtual maze for the unsuspecting officer, as they were the result of very little planning. After a number of wrong turns and dead ends, Ray finally found his way to room 204. The sign above the door read Computer Technology Services in brown block letters that had been recently painted on the well-worn hallway walls. Once inside, only one of the two computer technicians was visible.

Mitchell Edwards was a living, breathing caricature of a computer nerd, right down to the dreadful clothing. A color scheme was obviously not considered as a blue plaid shirt, buttoned to the neck, looked awful with the olive green slacks. To make it worse, the pants were about two inches too short, revealing a pair of mismatched socks. Horn-rimmed glasses held together with a strip of duct tape completed the ensemble. The only thing missing was a plastic pocket protector in the front of his shirt. Ray, biting his lip, kept himself in check.

Mitchell had Ray out the door in less than three minutes, armed with all the information he needed.

"Are you all set?" Dave asked Ray upon his return to the squad room.

Indicating his trip to the second floor had been successful, Ray answered, "You were right. They are amazing!"

Ray now had the addresses and phone numbers of Steve Brennan, Mark Schenck and Lawson Bramblett. Since Tucson's population swells in the winter with the arrival of midwestern snowbirds, Ray was relieved to find out that his three suspects were all local residents and were likely in town.

Because Nick Trikilos and Steve Brennan had made their reservations at the same time to play together on the day of Nick's death, Ray concluded that Steve was Nick's good-looking friend who, according to Donna, had left the Bar earlier in the afternoon. That meant that either Mark Schenck or Lawson Bramblett could possibly be Round Face—the last person to see Nick Trikilos alive and now Ray's prime suspect. Ray anxiously awaited the return of his captain, eager to share his discovery.

CHAPTER EIGHTEEN

WHILE MIKE GROMAN and Floyd LeRud made the short drive from Andreas Trikilos's office at 110 North Stone Avenue to the police station, they tried to decide whether their murder victim was Nick the Trick or Saint Nick. On one hand, they knew Nick Trikilos had been a street thug with loose ties to organized crime. On the other, Andreas Trikilos painted the picture of a churchgoing family man, one that gave noogies to his nephews and volunteered twice a week at Habitat for Humanity.

The truth was actually somewhere in between. Though he was of Athenian heritage, Nick was raised a Catholic and thoroughly embraced the religion. At the time he committed murder forty years earlier, he had considered his action to be retributive justice, but as he grew older, he became increasingly unable to reconcile his past with his spiritual principles. Nick had confessed his sins and received penance, but as he entered the autumn of his life, he privately feared the destination of his eternal soul.

Nick had become a different person after the Erin Kelly deal and was bewildered as to how a mortal sinner had become so financially blessed. Since he was unable to rewrite the past, he was determined to balance the ledger in the future. His sweat labor for Habitat for Humanity was cathartic, and working as a carpenter was unintentionally symbolic. In addition, and unbeknownst to anyone, he frequently made large anonymous cash donations to various charitable organizations, most often to Casa de los Niños, the Susan G. Komen Breast Cancer Foundation, and the American Heart Association. Some might believe that Nick Trikilos was trying to buy absolution, but his heart was in the right place. At the end of the day, Nick had become a decent and law-abiding person. His personalized license plate, NIKTRIK, was a constant reminder of his alter ego that always lurked and was a demon that he battled everyday.

It was 4:00 PM when Mike, Floyd, and Ray reunited in the squad room of the homicide unit. Ray was almost bursting with unbridled enthusiasm and exuberance when he said, "I think I know who killed Nick Trikilos."

Mike's experience told him that these types of cases were seldom solved this quickly or easily. It was with a great amount of skepticism that he asked his young detective, "So, who in the hell did it?"

Intrepidly, Ray answered, "It was one of two people." After pausing for dramatic affect, and somewhat annoying his impatient captain, Ray revealed the names of his suspects. "Lawson Bramblett or Mark Schenck."

Mike and Floyd simultaneously looked at each other because they recognized the name "Mark" from Steve Brennan's scorecard. Now with a peaked curiosity, Floyd asked, "Anything else?"

"Oh, yeah," Ray said with nonchalance, "I found the victim's car."

With that, Mike said to Ray, "Ten minutes. My office. Bring everything you've got."

Mike and Floyd had missed lunch that day, and they suddenly found themselves quite hungry. Floyd tagged along with his boss as they used the vending machines down the hall to buy a couple of Snickers bars and Diet Cokes. After using the restroom to freshen up, the two returned to Mike's office and an eager Ray Schrader.

The three of them were now ready to compare notes. Mike asked Ray, "Can you give me those two names again?"

Ray repeated, "Lawson Bramblett and Mark Schenck."

"How did you come up with those two names?"

Ray divulged his entire meeting with the four golf course employees, focusing particularly on the information provided by Donna Fulton, the manager of the Bar. He showed Mike and Floyd how he had used the reservation and tee time sheets to see who else was in the victim's foursome, and then confirmed that they had showed up to play golf that day by using their credit cards receipts.

For good measure, Ray added, "By the way, I've got their addresses and phone numbers."

"I see you found your way upstairs," said Mike, referring to the boys in Computer Technology Services.

Over the next half hour, by combining Steve Brennan's and Donna Fulton's recollections of the day's events, along with Ray's information, the three detectives were able to put together a possible scenario of the murder.

"Let me see if I've got this right," Mike began, as his two detectives took notes. "Nick Trikilos and Steve Brennan were joined by two single players, Lawson Bramblett and Mark Schenck, and began playing at 11:07 AM. At the conclusion of their round, at approximately 3:30 PM, the four entered the Bar and together ordered a couple of pitchers of beer, four glasses, and retreated to a table in the back of the room. At about 4:30 PM, Steve Brennan, who had dinner plans with his wife, left the Bar and was followed out shortly thereafter by Mark Schenck. Nick Trikilos and Lawson Bramblett remained long after the other two had left, with Nick getting bombed on bourbon. Now we don't know who this Lawson Bramblett is, but both Steve and Donna described this mystery guy as dark, heavy set and with a round face. Shortly after 7:00 PM, Donna briefly left the Bar and busied herself in the kitchen. When she returned, she assumed that everyone had left, so she turned off the lights, locked the door, and headed for the place of her gentleman du jour. Nick and our suspect were hiding somewhere inside, possibly back in the locker room or restroom. Lawson then dragged his drunken victim back into the Bar and beat him to death with a golf club. Do I pretty much have it?"

"That's right, Captain. So do you think this Lawson Bramblett could be our guy?" Ray asked.

"Well, it looks like our best bet right now. But, guys, try poking some holes in your theory." Mike already knew that there were some obvious problems, but this was more of an exercise for his two rookie detectives. He sat quietly for a moment and let Floyd and Ray take the initiative.

"First of all, the names on the scorecard were Nick, Steve, Mark and *Tony*, not Lawson," said Floyd. "How do you explain that?"

Unwilling to give an inch and thinking quickly, Ray answered, "If your name was Lawson Anthony Bramblett, wouldn't you go by Tony? What kind of name is Lawson?"

"Good point!" exclaimed Mike, impressed with his rookie detective. "Was there a middle initial on his credit card receipt?"

Ray pulled out the receipt and answered, "No, it just has Lawson Bramblett."

"What other problems do we have with our theory?" continued Mike.

"Well," said Ray, "we probably need some kind of a motive."

"When Nick got drunk, he probably said something that pissed off Tony, or Lawson, or whatever his name is," suggested Floyd.

"But to beat him to death with a golf club?" questioned Mike. "That's pretty fucking extreme."

Both Floyd and Ray were now at a loss.

"There's something that bothers me about the crime scene," said Floyd as he changed the subject. "Why was the broken glass from the door knocked *out* onto the walkway? How did that happen?"

The three detectives pondered this question for a few moments.

Finally Mike said, "It's been a long day, guys," realizing that the three were running out of gas in their brainstorming session. "You did a hell of a nice job today. We got a lot done. We'll pick up here tomorrow. We should be getting the autopsy and maybe some information from the TCSU. But first, we'll pay a visit to Lawson Bramblett."

That night on the five o'clock and ten o'clock local news, each station aired a brief story on the Nick Trikilos murder and investigation. Terry Bates, the public spokesperson for the Tucson Police Department, was interviewed and declined to divulge any details of the investigation. "We are following a number of investigative leads, but there is no other information we can release at this time." This was the standard, mundane response he always gave, which for some reason the local news stations always felt compelled to broadcast.

CHAPTER NINETEEN

ON FRIDAY MORNING, the *Arizona Daily Star* ran the following Nick Trikilos obituary using a picture that had been taken by his brother Andreas a few years earlier:

>Nicholas "Nick" Trikilos was suddenly taken from us on January 15th, less than one week before his 60th birthday. Born in Brooklyn, New York, Nick was preceded in death by his parents, Paulo and Leda (Trikilos). He is survived by his sister, Stephanie Trikilos Rodgers of Queens, N.Y., her husband, Ted, and their three children, Jamie, Ted Jr., and Alicia. Also mourning his death are his brother, Andreas, and his wife, Patty, and their children, Andre and Nick, all from Tucson. The immediate family is joined in sorrow by Nick's many friends and business partners. Nick called Tucson home since 1969. He was a prominent businessman and investor, but he will be best remembered for his charitable work with Habitat for Humanity, his love of golf, and the joy he brought to all he met. Services will be held on Saturday, January 19th at 10:00 AM at St. Pius Catholic Church immediately followed by his internment at Our Lady of the Desert Cemetery. In lieu of

flowers, donations may be made in Nick's memory to Habitat for Humanity or Casa de los Niños.

In addition to the obituary, Friday's paper also ran a lengthy story on Nick Trikilos that discussed his many business dealings, including the Erin Kelly poster story, and his extensive volunteer work. The piece also included a graphic description of Nick's violent death, the details undoubtedly provided by Sandy Wisconsin, who was only identified in the story as the golf course employee who discovered the body. As they would say in the news business, this story now had legs.

The previous day's rain had given way once again to cloudless blue skies. A ridge of high pressure had set up over the four corners area, where Arizona, New Mexico, Utah, and Colorado meet, and would raise the temperatures in Tucson to the midseventies. This unusually warm mid-January day is what the locals call "Chamber of Commerce weather," the kind of day that encourages winter visitors to stay longer or may even convince a midwestern business owner to relocate his company to the desert.

Winterhaven is the name of an older subdivision of well-kept homes located in Tucson's near north side. For the past sixty years at Christmas time, the residents of Winterhaven have lavishly adorned their homes with holiday decorations, from the tasteful to the absurd, competing for prizes in a contest sponsored by their homeowners association. The Tucson Electric Power Company contributes to the event by sending out a crew to cover the many streetlights with candy canes, garland, and wreathes. In the evening, families from all over the city make their annual pilgrimage to take in the sights and sounds of this winter wonderland, traversing the streets named North Pole Avenue, Santa's Way, and Christmas Tree Place. A can of food for the Community Food Bank is the price of admission.

It was 9:00 AM when Mike, Floyd, and Ray pulled up to 7314 Christmas Tree Place, the address of Lawson Bramblett's home.

The three detectives sat quietly in the car for a few moments as they watched a man hanging precariously from the top of a ladder, removing a string of holiday lights from the fascia of his home. He was probably the last resident of Winterhaven to do so. He was wearing a green Arizona Fertilizer hat, a dingy white tee shirt with a large yellow silk-screened picture of the cartoon character Tweety Bird on the front, and a pair of what appeared to be blue flannel pajama bottoms. After watching this clown nearly fall twice, Mike rhetorically asked his two partners, "Who in the fuck is *this* guy?"

Leaving their car and approaching their suspect who was almost suspended in midair, Mike called up, "Are you Lawson Bramblett?"

"Who wants to know?" came a snippy reply from above.

"We're the police. We'd like to ask you a few questions."

After apologizing for his somewhat rude response, Lawson Bramblett made his way down the ladder, removed his two old work gloves, and shook hands with the three detectives.

Lawson Bramblett was a sixty-something retired middle school teacher. Tall and slender, he had a full head of gray hair that gave every indication that at one time he had been a blonde. The three detectives did not need Sherlock Holmes to tell them that Lawson Delbert Bramblett was not their Round Face Tony.

After the introductions, Lawson asked, "How can I help you guys?"

"We are investigating the death of Nick Trikilos," said Mike, assuming that the media coverage had made any other information unnecessary. His assumption was correct.

"I read about him in the paper this morning and saw something on TV," said Lawson.

Mike continued, "The information we have says that on Tuesday you were scheduled to play in a foursome with him, but we don't think you did. Can you tell us what happened?"

"Wow! Do you mean one of those guys was the one that got killed?"

"So, can you tell us what happened?"

"Sure. I was put with these three other guys, and we were supposed to tee off at a little after eleven. I was stopped by some guy who offered me twenty bucks to trade times with him so he could play with his good friend in my group. His tee time was only fifteen minutes later, so I told him that would be fine. I didn't even take his money."

"Can you describe the man you traded tee times with?" asked Mike.

"He was about five-foot-ten-inch tall, maybe fifty-five or sixty years old, kind of heavy with dark hair and a very round face," answered Lawson.

It had now become absurd to the three detectives to hear almost the exact same description given over and over and over again by complete strangers.

"Can you tell us anything else?" asked Captain Groman.

Lawson finished by answering, "I teed off at about 11:30 and played like crap. I never saw any of them again."

"Did you go into the Bar when you finished your round of golf?"

"No, I just returned the golf cart, went to the parking lot, and then headed home."

"Do you think you would recognize that round-faced man again?" inquired Mike.

"Sure, I think so."

"Would you be willing to come downtown to the police station and help our sketch artists make a composite drawing of this round-faced guy?"

"Do you guys think that he might be the killer?" asked Lawson.

Without answering, Mike simply said, "It would be a big help."

"Heck, I'm retired with nothing more pressing to do than take down these lights. I've seen those sketch artists on *Law & Order*. It will be kind of interesting to see how they really work. When do you want me to head down?"

"Go ahead and finish your job here," answered Mike. "After lunch will be just fine. Do you know where to go?"

"I know where the main police station is downtown."

"Just go in the main entrance and see the sergeant at the front desk. I'll let him know that you are coming in. He'll escort you—its kind of hard finding your way around the place."

The three officers thanked Lawson for his help and cooperation, and then filed back into their unmarked police car. Mike climbed behind the wheel, while Floyd rode shotgun, and Ray sat in the rear. Before starting the car, the three officers sat quietly for a few seconds, digesting the information from the interview. Collectively, they were disappointed that Lawson Bramblett was not Round Face Tony.

Then from the backseat, Ray said, "Delbert?"

The three broke into laughter as Mike started the car and drove off.

CHAPTER TWENTY

AFTER RETURNING FROM the Bramblett residence, Mike pulled into his reserved parking space at the Tucson Police Station and left his car running as he addressed his two detectives. "Now we've got four people who can identify Round Face Tony. There's Nick's friend Steve Brennan, the manager of the Bar, Lawson Bramblett, and Mark Schenck, who we still have to contact. I want all four of them down here this afternoon to work with the sketch artist. The more people who have input, the more accurate the composite tends to be." Then, Mike ended his instructions by informing his two detectives for the first time that he needed to leave. "I'm heading over to the coroner's office, and I'm not sure how long I'll be. Make sure you take Mark Schenck's statement while he's here if I don't make it back."

It was clear to Mike that Mark Schenck would probably have very little to add to what they already knew. He was merely the final member of the foursome who had played golf, shared a beer, and would be able to help identify Round Face Tony.

Before he left, Mike asked, "Floyd, what was the name of that guy that Andreas Trikilos said had a beef with his brother?"

"The last name was Reep. His first name was something like Gary or Jerry, I think. I have it in my desk."

"If you have time, see what you can find out about him," said Mike. He then dismissed Floyd and Ray from his car, leaving them to decide how best to carry out their missions. "Make it happen," Mike said.

Mike was now headed to the Pima County coroner's office where they had performed the autopsy on Nick Trikilos. Their office was located south of the city and close to the Tucson International Airport, an easy twenty-minute drive from the police station. This normally pleasurable ride was made more so by the gorgeous weather that Mike enjoyed with his rolled-down windows.

Claire Pontius was one of the few female medical examiners in the United States. For a myriad of possible reasons, her job mainly attracted men who resembled the actor Jack Klugman, who portrayed an aging coroner on the seventies TV show, *Quincy, M.E.* Claire was no Jack Klugman. The petite twenty-nine-year-old blonde with dazzling blue eyes and an engaging smile, had exceptional skills as a medical examiner in spite of only three years of experience.

Even though Mike was some thirty years her senior, the two, nonetheless, enjoyed engaging in a flirtatious banter every time Mike entered her office.

"So, Claire," Mike said as she looked up from her work, "what do you say we head down to Cabo for the weekend?"

"Oh, Mike," she coyly responded, "we'd spend so much time traveling, why don't we just hit the No Tell Motel?" (Believe it or not, Tucson actually has a No Tell Motel, located on a street called Miracle Mile.)

Unable to come to a compromise concerning their weekend plans, Mike got down to business by asking Claire, "What can you tell me about my boy Nick Trikilos?"

She handed Mike a file containing over thirty pictures of the victim and his wounds taken from every conceivable angle. After a careful examination of each one, Mike began reading the three-page report that detailed each lesion and eventually determined the exact cause of death.

With a chagrined look on his face, he handed the file back to Claire and asked, "Would you please translate all of this medical mumbo jumbo?"

Mike had performed this exact same ritual many times before, even asking the same question verbatim.

Fully prepared, Claire secured the folder and thumbed through its pages as she offered a simpler rendition.

"Nick Trikilos was a sixty-year-old male of Mediterranean descent." Pausing as she quickly converted the metric to standard, she continued, "He was five-feet-nine inches tall and weighed 158 lbs. He was probably unaware of the beginning stages of cirrhoses of the liver, but overall was in relatively good health. The little blood that he had left contained an alcohol level of .214."

After the rather formal introduction of her report, Claire summarized the remainder of her findings in Gromanese by saying "He was bombed! With that much booze in him, he was probably barely able to walk. He got into a fight and was beaten like a red-headed stepchild. He had glass fragments stuck in his head from being used as a human battering ram when he was thrust through a plate glass door."

Mike now understood how the broken glass ended up *outside* the Bar on the walkway.

"In this collision," Claire continued, "his left ear was nearly severed by a knifelike piece of broken glass. At this point, the victim in all likelihood was unconscious and then dragged back into the Bar. We came to that conclusion from the smeared blood on the carpet and the matching carpet fibers on his forehead. He was then finished off with five distinct blows to the head with a golf club, a Ping Eye 2, a seven iron. The head of the club remained imbedded in his shattered skull after the fifth and final blow."

"Can you tell me anything about the seven iron?" Mike asked.

"Your CSU will have all of that in their report," said Claire. "All I can tell you is that the golf club was the lethal weapon . . . a first for me."

Meanwhile, Floyd and Ray were semisuccessful in carrying out their captain's orders. Back at the police station, Lawson Bramblett showed up shortly after 1:00 PM as promised. He immediately began working with Floyd and Big Jim Walker, a personable and highly skilled police sketch artist.

The Bar at the Randolph Golf Complex had an uneventful grand reopening that day, with both new carpeting and a replaced glass door.

As usual, Sandy opened that morning and was scheduled to work until 1:00 PM when she would be relieved by Donna Fulton. Because the police needed Donna's help downtown, Sandy, who had not worked for three days, was more than happy to pull a double shift. Donna joined Lawson, Floyd, and Big Jim Walker shortly after 1:15 PM.

Five minutes later, Steve Brennan also arrived, as he could easily leave Fitz in the capable hands of his assistants at any time and for any duration.

Without taking a break, the three witnesses worked with Floyd and the sketch artist until a few minutes before 3:00 PM. Steve, Donna, and Lawson left feeling very satisfied with their work and agreed that their composite drawing accurately depicted Round Face Tony.

Corralling Mark Schenck was more problematic. When Floyd and Ray arrived at Mark's home earlier that morning, his wife Jessica informed them that Mark was chosen for jury duty and had been serving since Wednesday, which was the day after the murder. He had been selected to sit on a trial that was expected to last about a week. Other than that, Jessica had no other details to offer because, as she said, "Mark was instructed by the judge not to discuss the case with anyone," and he took the judge's admonition very seriously.

Floyd remained back at the police station to assist the three witnesses with their drawing as Ray waited patiently outside Superior Courtroom 6. Because it was Friday, the jury was dismissed at 3:45 PM for the weekend and instructed to return on Monday at 8:30 AM. Ray intercepted Mark as he was quickly heading for the exit and briefly explained to him the situation.

Mark Schenck was a retired United States Army Colonel, a graduate of West Point, with an expertise in computers and computer software. He left the armed forces after twenty years of service, the military's earliest opportunity for retirement, and began a successful software business out of his home. He was forty-eight years old and the father of four girls, two of whom were in college. Although he was a computer nerd, his outward appearance did not reflect his profession, unlike Mitchell Edwards in Computer Technology Services back at the police station.

Because the municipal parking lot was located halfway between the Superior Court Building and the police station, Mark decided to leave his car and walk the four short blocks, happy to be outside in the fresh air.

Upon arriving at the station, Mark Schenck was quickly interviewed by Mike, who had returned from the coroner's office. Mike was satisfied that, as expected, this witness had nothing to do with Nick's murder. Then, after seeing the composite drawing of their prime suspect Round Face Tony, Mark exclaimed, "That's him! My God, it could be a photograph!"

CHAPTER TWENTY-ONE

POLICE CHIEF GEORGE Sladek was a fourth generation police officer who felt he had reached the summit of his profession and had no real ambition, political or otherwise, to advance his career. He was a demanding administrator who appreciated excellence and would not tolerate mediocrity. He neither gave nor accepted excuses, he treated people fairly, and when fighting the city council for funding, he gave no quarter. The chief took pride in his department, and in the tradition of the western lawman, he planned on being carried out of his office one day, still wearing his cowboy boots.

Chief Sladek's phone call to Mike interrupted the Captain's regularly scheduled late Friday afternoon meeting with his five detectives—Jeff Green, Steve Kraus, Bob Stewart, Sandra Lara, and Dave Starbuck. They were in the process of updating their captain on the status of their current investigations, as Jeff Green had just announced the arrest of a suspect in the Blas Vargas case, which was a particularly gruesome murder that had remained unsolved for over two years.

"Good afternoon, Mike, it's George," said the chief who always started his conversation with Mike the same way, except for changing the time of day. "Do you have time to talk?"

Mike knew that when his boss called, he was expected to make time. "No problem, George, what can I do for you?"

Mike's detectives immediately realized that the caller was the chief of police and promptly excused themselves from his office. They spent the final half hour of their work week cleaning up various reports.

With the pleasantries out of the way, George asked, "What can you give me on the Nick Trikilos case?"

Mike Groman spent the next few minutes catching his boss up to speed about the evidence his team had gathered and the information that he and his detectives had gleaned from their interviews. Mike also informed George what he anticipated to be the future direction of the case.

"Is there anything I can do to help?" asked the chief.

Mike understood that this question was a blank check offer of departmental administrative resources. "The only thing I really need is the report from the CSU. I thought I would have it by today."

Because it was so late in the day on Friday, George promised what he could. "It will be on your desk when you walk in Monday morning. Is there anything else you need?" George's promise would mean that the CSU would be working late into the night, and probably most of the weekend.

Requesting nothing else, Mike ended his call with George Sladek by briefly discussing the National Football League playoff games that would be contested that weekend. The two placed a friendly wager on the outcome of the game between the Dallas Cowboys and the New York Giants. Mike and his live-in mother-in-law, Mim, were huge Cowboys fans and always enjoyed watching their games together.

Captain Groman made a point of verbally recognizing the achievements of those in his charge. Unlike the first-grade teacher who passes out gold stars for every child's minimal effort, Mike, like his boss, rewarded excellence. Jeff Green had recently been the recipient of such recognition for his outstanding work in the Blas Vargas case.

Mike played football in high school for the legendary Doug Sale. What separated coach Sale from his peers was his unique ability to motivate every player to practice and play to their fullest potential. Not every player was a star, but everyone felt like one. Mike modeled his approach to his supervisory duties after his coach's approach to motivating a football team because he knew that his detectives would go the extra mile if they felt their work was appreciated.

He finished the week by calling Floyd and Ray back into his office for a brief meeting.

"I want to thank you two for working with me on this case," Mike said, emphasizing the word *with*, and fully aware that his two detectives were thrilled to have been given this opportunity to work on such a high profile case with the captain of the homicide unit.

He continued by telling them he was very happy with their work over the past three days, and then he outlined their plan for the upcoming week.

"Although you are both here only temporarily, I hope someday you apply for detective, that is, if this is the type of police work that you like. I think you two would be good ones." Then Mike added, "You know, not every cop can become a good detective. Many that I've known couldn't pour piss out of a boot with the directions on the heel."

That night on the evening news, the local TV stations displayed Big Jim Walker's work—the sketch of Round Face Tony. He was described as a five-foot-ten-inch tall, two-hundred-pound, and fifty-to-sixty-year-old *person of interest* in the Nick Trikilos homicide investigation. The public was instructed to call the Tucson Police Tip Hotline or 911 if they had any information as to his identity or whereabouts.

Meanwhile, 350 miles to the west in San Diego, California, television station KTSD broadcasted an exclusive live report from the Del Mar Race Track where an unidentified man was found dead in the parking lot, apparently beaten to death with a golf club. The reporter on the scene was unsuccessful in obtaining a statement from the police.

CHAPTER TWENTY-TWO

THE MURDER OF my second victim, unlike my first, went like clockwork. The reconnaissance that I did three months earlier paid dividends, as this subject proved to be a creature of habit.

After Labor Day, the Del Mar Race Track closes for the season. Then, every Friday, the parking lot is turned into a giant farmers market, where fresh produce from all over southern California is sold at bargain prices. The vendors begin selling their goods at eight o'clock, although they don't start getting busy until ten.

Back in October, my target, Dominic Cirillo, arrived promptly at nine o'clock and parked his car in a secluded part of the lot. Why, I don't know. I then watched him carry a large canvas bag and make the long walk to where the merchants were located, shop for about an hour, and return to his car for the two-mile drive back to his home. He repeated this exact same ritual three weeks in a row.

On this Friday, I arrived at the racetrack at seven thirty sharp. I wanted to be early in the event that Dominic Cirillo had changed his routine. I took my position near the Pacific Coast Highway, some hundred yards away, though in full view of where I expected him to park his car. And then I waited.

At nine o'clock on the button, as if on cue, he pulled his Lexus SUV into the exact same spot as he had done before. I watched him march toward the marketplace, with what looked like the same canvas bag he had used back in October. It took him almost ten minutes to walk and then disappear in and among the hundreds of merchants.

I then pulled my car around and parked about fifty yards from his Lexus, in the direct line he would need to take to get back to his vehicle. At five minutes to ten, I watched Dominic Cirillo begin his long walk back to his car.

I was standing outside and leaning up against my black Lincoln Town Car as he walked past. We even exchanged a brief greeting. I must have looked like a chauffeur, waiting for his client. He was carrying a sack of groceries in one hand and a bouquet of flowers in the other.

As soon as he went by, I immediately took one final look around to see that no one was in the area. Satisfied that we were alone in this deserted section of the parking lot, I reached through the opened window of my sedan and grabbed my five iron. I took about ten quick steps toward my retreating target and dropped him with one fierce blow to the side of his head. Unlike Nick Trikilos, Dominic Cirillo literally never knew what hit him. Judging from his wound, it was obvious that he would not survive this attack, that is if he wasn't already dead.

I dropped the golf club to the ground among the groceries and flowers, which were now scattered about my victim. Within a minute, I was back in my car, leaving the parking lot, and heading south on the Pacific Coast Highway.

This had been a busy four days. I killed Nick Trikilos in Tucson on Tuesday and Dominic Cirillo in Del Mar on Friday. I can't help but think that Dad will be proud of my accomplishments. Two down and two to go.

CHAPTER TWENTY-THREE

THE PARKING LOT at St. Pius Catholic Church on Saturday morning was about three quarters full when Mike Groman arrived at 9:45 AM for the funeral of Nick Trikilos. Wearing one of the two suits he owned, Mike attended the funeral for two reasons: to pay his respects to the family and more importantly, to try and figure out from the other attendees who exactly Nickolas Trikilos was. He felt that this information might possibly prove useful in his investigation. Parked in the main driveway of the church were six matching black limousines and a hearse from Bring's Funeral Home.

It was quite an eclectic group that had gathered inside the sanctuary. Mike immediately recognized Andreas Trikilos, Nick's older brother whom he had interviewed on Thursday. Seated next to him in the front center pew, Mike assumed, was his very attractive wife Patty and their two sons, Andre and Nick. Seated next to them at the right of center, Mike judged from the strong family resemblance, was the youngest of the Trikilos' siblings, Stephanie, with her husband Ted. Mike found out later that the two had just flown in the night before from their home in New York, leaving behind their three older children who were never very close to their uncle Nick.

Just as the service was about to begin, Mike took his seat toward the rear of the sanctuary, while other mourners continued to file in behind him. Looking out over a sea of black, Mike spotted Nick's golfing partner and friend Steve Brennan, who was seated presumably with his wife about five rows from the front. Other than the recognizable immediate family and the Brennans, everyone else was a stranger to Mike.

Except for one elegant floral arrangement placed next to the closed casket, the family's wishes for donations to Nick's favorite charities in his honor were appreciatively respected.

Mike anticipated an eloquent and emotional eulogy to be delivered by Andreas Trikilos, and Andreas did not disappoint, although it was of an uncomfortable length. He was followed by one of Nick's business partners who spoke of Nick's integrity, and then by the director of the local Habitat for Humanity who spoke of Nick's charitableness. Following the eulogy was a full mass that included numerous readings and prayers that were appropriate for the occasion. Father Thompson spoke very kindly of the deceased, whom he had known for years, and offered spiritual comfort to Nick's family and friends. Later, Mike would be engaged by the good father as he exited the sanctuary, who would ask politely how he had known Nick. Mike would explain that he was investigating Nick's murder, but would leave out the details of how their paths had crossed over twenty years earlier.

But for now, Mike remained seated during communion and watched intently as the mourners lined up to receive the sacrament. Each recipient shared the same solemn expression as they slowly moved through the communion line and eventually returned to their seats. Unbeknownst to Mike, passing by his right shoulder from his aisle seat was Salvatore "Little Sal" Giambi, the nephew of the late Joseph Bonnano. For a short time following the retirement of the elder Bonnano, Salvatore had become the head of what was left of the original Bonnano crime family.

After the service, Mike made his way outside to where Andreas and Stephanie were standing and offered them and their families his sincerest condolences. The three briefly commented on the beautiful service. Andreas Trikilos was very surprised to see Captain Groman at the funeral but was nonetheless appreciative of his appearance and support. After introducing Captain Groman to his sister, Andreas turned to Mike with one simple request: "Please find who did this to my brother."

Mike did not accompany the procession that made its way to Our Lady of the Desert Cemetery for the internment of Nick Trikilos. Instead, on his drive home from the church, Mike loosened his tie and played back in his mind the words of those who had spoken of Nick during the service. Mike was beginning to believe that Nick *may* have actually changed over the years and that Andreas's portrayal of his brother was an accurate depiction of the murder victim.

CHAPTER TWENTY-FOUR

MIKE GROMAN WALKED into the squad room Monday morning, looking as though his hair had been entangled in a KitchenAid Mix Master. Outside, a powerful and dangerous storm was hammering the western United States. California had already been pummeled with torrential rains that caused mudslides in areas charred by summer wildfires. Tucson, while remaining dry, received sustained winds of thirty miles per hour with wind gusts of up to fifty. Cities to the north, as close as Phoenix, were pounded with flooding rains while the higher elevations from Flagstaff to Denver experienced blizzard conditions. Cities to the east prepared for the worst.

It was still surprising to everyone in the squad room that Mike's hair was affected at all by the stiff wind. His detectives good naturedly joked that their captain's hair never met a tube of Brylcreem it didn't like.

After pulling himself together and starting his coffeemaker, Mike began looking through the CSU folder that, as promised by the chief of police, was now on his desk.

The first part of the report was devoted to fingerprints. The Bar was a public restaurant, so it contained literally hundreds of viable prints. The CSU had painstakingly run about half of them through their computer system and promised the other half by the end of the day. They sought to identify anyone in the system with a criminal or violent past who could be investigated as a possible suspect. Of all the prints, only nineteen matched individuals in the system. Fourteen of those belonged to either current or former public school employees who were required by law to be printed as a condition of employment. Members of the law enforcement community accounted for four others, while the remaining print was that of a Hector Ruiz, who was booked back in 1998 on an aggravated DUI.

"No one very interesting here," Mike said to himself.

The second section of the report analyzed the DNA evidence collected at the scene. The CSU compiled this evidence from countless hair follicles found in the Bar, as well as bodily fluids from the restrooms that were not kept in the most sanitary of conditions. If the CSU was given a suspect's DNA, a match would at least place him at the scene. This alone would not guarantee a conviction but could be an important piece of the overall puzzle.

Blood was seemingly sprayed everywhere in the Bar, as the furthest samples were taken 9.6 meters apart, or almost thirty feet. Blood samples were also recovered from the pieces of broken glass on the walkway leading out from the Bar, along with larger jagged pieces that had not been dislodged from the shattered door. Mike realized this evidence was consistent with the coroner's report. The majority of the blood was found in a large pool beneath the victim's head, most of which had been absorbed by the carpet. Each carefully examined blood sample—every spec—belonged to only one person: the victim Nick Trikilos.

Information on the murder weapon, the Ping Eye 2 seven iron, was contained in the final section of the report. The murder weapon had a steel shaft, as compared to graphite, with the serial number 14684 carved into the housel, which is where the end of the shaft meets the head of club. It had a rubber grip that had been covered in blood, except for where the murderer's hand wrapped tightly around the grip, which gave the appearance that the blood had been stenciled around the murderer's handprint. More significantly, there were no discernible fingerprints anywhere on the club.

Golfers are limited to fourteen clubs in their bag. They are allowed to carry less, but not more. There is almost an infinite number of possible combinations of clubs that a golfer can choose for his specific type of game, but the average golfer will carry three woods, seven irons, three wedges, and a putter.

The woods of today are, in reality, a misnomer. Decades ago, these clubs were handcrafted out of a hardwood called persimmon, from a tree that produces a reddish orange edible fruit. Today, however, these same clubs are made out of space-aged polymers and titanium. Whether those in the business were unable to come up with a new name or simply had a desire to preserve history, the term *wood* has remained to this day. A three-club set of woods is typically comprised of a driver, a three wood, and a five wood. Striking a golf ball with either of the three, in best cases, sends the spheroid a great distance and the differences of the three can be seen in the ball's trajectory.

The irons, usually numbered three through nine, are used when a shot requires a shorter distance but greater accuracy.

The various wedges are used for finesse shots near and around the putting surface.

But most golfers agree the most important club in the bag is the one that hits the ball the shortest distance: the putter. This club ultimately knocks the ball into the hole, and the difference between a good round of golf and a poor one is often determined by the number of times this club is used.

With the vast amount of evidence to analyze, Mike now understood why he did not have the CSU report on Friday as he had hoped. He was now sympathetic and appreciative of the CSU, knowing they had put in considerable overtime this past weekend. He made a mental note to remember to thank them and to apologize for involving the chief of police.

Mike finished reviewing the report at the same time he finished his third cup of coffee. On his way to the men's room, he was stopped by Floyd who said, "Good morning, Captain, how was your weekend?"

Ray, who was seated at an adjoining desk, asked, "Captain, are you all right?" He posed his question before Mike had a chance to answer Floyd.

Not knowing that Ray was referring to his still somewhat disheveled appearance caused by his brief walk in the wind, Mike answered, "I better have my prostate checked," adding, "that coffee ran through me like shit through a goose."

Before continuing his trek to the men's room, Mike instructed Floyd to go to room 109, which housed the community liaison office. There, he was to pick up any tips that may have been phoned in following the broadcast of Round Face Tony's composite, which had aired both Friday and Saturday nights.

"Let's meet back in my office in ten minutes," said Mike, as he walked off with a sense of urgency.

CHAPTER TWENTY-FIVE

MIKE GAVE COPIES of the CSU report to Floyd and Ray as the two entered his office. After allowing the detectives a few moments to digest the contents of the report, Mike interrupted their review by giving them their assignments for the day.

"Floyd, I need you to follow up on those tips that came in over the weekend about the possible whereabouts of Round Face Tony," Mike began.

The police officers, who manned the tip hotline over the weekend after the media released the composite sketch of Round Face Tony, had received some bizarre phone calls. "I was stopped at a red light at Grant Road and Columbus Avenue, and a guy that looked just like him walked right out in front of me. I almost hit him!" These types of calls are what the officers at the Tucson Police Department would classify as a "UFO," or a "useless fucking observation." Such calls were politely dismissed as the paperwork documenting the call was filed in an appropriate receptacle. Other calls clearly had nothing to do with the case—one was payback from an upset girlfriend who just wanted the police to hassle her boyfriend, even though he looked nothing like the picture. Sadly, there was even one call from a lonely old soul, without family or friends, who desperately craved any type of human contact.

However, there were a number of calls that would require further investigation. The community liaison office had turned the records of these calls over to Floyd just a few moments earlier.

Mike chose Floyd for this assignment in part because he felt that Floyd might conduct interviews more aptly than his partner Ray. He also felt that Floyd had a better temperament to handle the frustration of following what could turn out to be countless dead ends, which was often par for the course for this type of police work.

Mike believed that Ray, on the other hand, would use his bulldog determination to take a simple task and see it through to completion without missing the slightest detail.

"Ray, I need you to find out everything there is to know about our murder weapon—the Ping Eye 2 seven iron. Talk to Mr. Fucking Ping himself if you need to, but I want to know everything about that golf club."

After giving his rookie detectives their assignments, Mike said, "Call if you have any questions or if you need my help." Mike would spend the better part of the day behind his desk, catching up on his administrative duties that he had let slide in the excitement of returning to the field in this brand new murder investigation.

Floyd exited Mike's office, eager to begin tracking down the potential leads that had come in over the weekend. Ray, on the other hand, unsure of where to begin yet wanting to appear confident, was hesitant in asking his captain for further direction.

"Captain, I was thinking of going back to the golf course to ask the head pro about the golf club," Ray offered. "He might be able to at least give me some of the basics."

"Good idea," Mike responded encouragingly. "What was his name again?"

"Don Weber."

"Oh yeah," said Mike, "Weber . . . one B . . . just like the grill. What a dick."

On a normal day, the parking lot at the Randolph Golf Complex would nearly be filled by 9:00 AM. On this day, however, fewer golfers had chosen to brave the elements than even those who had done so on Thursday, indicating that golfers detest the wind more so than the rain.

With very little business, Don Weber was more than happy to spend time with Ray Schrader, while Pete watched the store. With the greetings out of the way, Ray and Don headed back to the office of the head professional.

"What can you tell me about the Ping Eye 2 golf club?" Ray began.

"Well, how much do you know about golf?" Don wanted to know about the officer's pre-existing knowledge of clubs and the game, because this would help him determine how best to answer his questions.

Ray understood the motive behind Don's inquiry without any explanation. "I get out about a half dozen times a year, so I wouldn't call myself a golfer, but with a mulligan or two, I usually break 100."

"What kind of clubs do you use?"

"My girlfriend bought me a set of Callaways for our first anniversary. I think she was trying to prove that she didn't mind me spending time with the guys."

"Callaways are nice clubs," Don said casually, now aware that he was not speaking to an absolute novice.

"I should have had them custom fit. With my height, or lack of it, I think I ended up with clubs that are too long."

"Why don't you bring them in and see what I can do."

"I'll do that, thanks," Ray said appreciatively. "But getting back to those Pings, what can you tell me?"

Because of Ray's ample understanding of the game, Don was able to impart his knowledge about this particular brand of golf club to the officer without having to explain every slightest detail.

"Although this may not be 100 percent accurate," Don began as Ray took out his notepad, "the story of Ping Golf began back in the late sixties or early seventies."

Don Weber told his captive audience the interesting story of how an engineer with one of the oldest and largest club makers, a company that feared innovation, decided to quit and head out on his own. Throwing out all conventions, he designed what he felt was the perfect putter. He enlisted numerous golfers to field test his prototype, which he built in his garage. Their positive feedback was overwhelmingly enthusiastic. The putter did, however, make an unusual sound when it struck the ball, which almost sounded like a tuning fork used on a piano, possibly an F sharp. The onomatopoetic Ping Putter was born. This new club was an immediate success locally in the Phoenix area, but when the inventor was able to convince a few golfers on the PGA Tour to try it, the demand soon spread nationwide.

"Unable to keep up with the orders from his garage, he opened up a factory in the midseventies, and as they say, the rest is history." Don concluded his story with the disclaimer: "As near as I can recall, that's how Ping Golf began."

"So when did they move from just putters to manufacturing a full line of golf clubs?"

"That I don't recall, sometime back in the late seventies I think. But I do remember exactly when the Ping Eye 2 model came out." Don confidently continued, "It was 1988."

"How are you so sure of the year?"

"I purchased a set of those for my son Greg's sixteenth birthday. They had just hit the market, and they had a real nice feel to them."

Ray asked Don to provide him with more information specifically about the murder weapon—the seven iron, which had a serial number on the housel.

"The top manufacturers number their clubs so that if one is lost or stolen, the company can replace it with an exact replica—same length, weight, loft, and lie," explained Don. "Your clubs are also numbered. If you have the serial number of the murder weapon, I can contact Ping and find out who originally purchased those clubs."

An excited Ray Schrader, who did not expect this much help, said, "Wow! That would be great if you could. I've got the number right here. How long will it take?"

Don reached for his phone and directory. "I'll call right now. What's the serial number?"

Ray wrote the number 14684 on a slip of paper while Don called Jeff Scott, one of the top executives of Ping Golf, on his direct line.

"Hey, Jeff, it's Don." After a brief pause, Don cordially said, "Good, how about you?"

After the brief exchange of pleasantries, Don cut to the chase. "Jeff, what can you tell me about an Eye 2, serial number fourteen-six-eighty-four?" Pausing again, Don repeated the serial number more clearly. "One, four, six, eight, four . . . sure, I can wait."

Don turned to Ray and told him that Jeff was having his secretary pull the information up on their computer. He then grabbed a pen and a piece of paper and began scribbling some notes. Don then ended the call by saying, "Thanks, Jeff, for all of your help. Let's play the next time you come down."

Don listened to Jeff on the other end for a few moments and then said, "Sure thing, Jeff, and thanks again. Give my best to Debbie. All right . . . Bye."

Don handed Ray the note he had written:

> Thomas Sanford
> c/o The Oakwood Country Club
> 1362 E. Fairway Drive
> Indianapolis, Indiana
> 46203
> Ping Eye 2 Irons, 1-9, P, S
> Shipped Jan. 8, 1989

This set of golf clubs, because it included both the one and two irons, was very unusual. Except for a handful of pros, like Tiger Woods, very few golfers are able to use these couple of clubs successfully and with any consistency. Most recreational golfers replace them with the much easier to hit three and five woods.

The P and the S on Don's note stood for "pitching wedge" and "sand wedge" respectively, both of which, along with the remaining clubs, were very common.

Don took a few minutes and explained to Ray how odd it was for a set of clubs to contain both the one and two irons. Ray fully understood and replied that when he played golf, the nine iron was the easiest club to hit and that the difficulty progressed with each lower number. To Ray, an occasional golfer, successfully hitting a four iron bordered on impossible. He could only imagine how thorny the game would become if he had to use a one or a two iron.

Don always had a story for every occasion. He couldn't help but share with Ray one of his favorites, which coincidentally pertained to Ray's investigation of this unusual set of Pings.

"While four golfers were playing one day in a high stakes game, storm clouds were brewing and moving very quickly into the area. Soon, the sirens on the course sounded, a warning to all of the golfers to seek shelter immediately, as lightning was detected in the vicinity. But because this was a big money game, and since the golfers only had two holes to go, they proceeded on. By the time they reached the eighteenth tee, the storm was directly overhead—hail, thunder, lightning, and high winds. The four huddled around a nearby tree, seeking shelter, but each knew that this was too dangerous, as lightning strikes the tallest object in the area. Meanwhile, the golfers that had used good judgment were now in the clubhouse enjoying a beverage while they watched these four idiots by the eighteenth tee huddled around the giant oak. One of the four golfers decided to make a mad dash to the clubhouse. Down the fairway he raced, dodging lightning strikes to the left, then the right. Halfway to safety, he was struck and laid motionless in the middle of the fairway in the driving rain, to the horror of those watching from the clubhouse. The second golfer took his chances, followed immediately by the third. Although they both made it farther than the first pioneer, each met the same fate. Now with three bodies strewn across the eighteenth fairway, the fourth and final member of group reached into his bag, pulled out his two iron, and holding it straight up in the air as high as he could, calmly walked right down the middle of the fairway, with lightning striking all around him, and untouched into the clubhouse. The cheering crowd inside that witnessed this feat welcomed the lone survivor with towels to dry and bourbon to calm his nerves. One of the witnesses couldn't help but ask, 'Why did you hold that club high over your head as you walked so calmly to the clubhouse, particularly after you witnessed the fate of your friends?' The shivering rain-soaked golfer peered out from beneath a towel draped over his head and simply said, 'Even God can't hit a two iron!'"

While Ray had great success in his meeting with Don Weber, his partner Floyd had spent the morning out of the office and spinning his wheels. Monday, January 21, was the birthday of Nick Trikilos and also the day the country chose to commemorate the birthday of Dr. Martin Luther King Jr. Because of the holiday, many people were off from work, so Floyd was able to contact nine of the eleven tipsters who believed they had information concerning the location of Round Face Tony. Floyd methodically eliminated one look-alike after another and would continue doing so for most of the day.

Ray arrived back at the squad room and immediately called the Oakwood Country Club in Indianapolis, Indiana. He asked for Thomas Sanford, and although the receptionist explained that Mr. Sanford was a member of their private club, she said she hadn't seen him that day. After Ray briefly explained the nature of his call, she suggested he talk to the head golf pro, Rick Held, who might be able to help him.

The transferred call was almost immediately answered. "Hi, Rick Held."

Ray repeated the purpose of his call and asked about Thomas Sanford.

"Tommy is one heck of a nice guy. He bought those Ping Eye 2s about twenty years back when Mike Piekarski was the head pro here."

"Do you know if Mr. Sanford is still playing with those clubs?"

"I finally talked him into a new set of clubs about two years ago. Just between you and me, if everyone was as cheap as Tommy, we'd go broke. Many of our members replace their clubs every year."

"Do you know if he still has his old set of clubs?"

"No, I mean he might have them stored somewhere for nostalgic sake, but I couldn't say for sure. Look, Tommy's one of the most upstanding guys I know. I'm sure he didn't have anything to do with this murder you're investigating, and I'm also sure he'd be glad to help you out in any way that he can. I'd be happy to give you his phone number, and you can talk to him yourself."

Ray finished the call by thanking the head golf pro at the Oakwood Country Club for his help and thanking him for Tommy Sanford's cell number.

Tommy Sanford was born in Montgomery, Alabama, and although his family moved to Indianapolis when he was quite young, he retained the slightest hint of a southern drawl. His protruding angular jaw would be the focal point of a caricaturist, although women generally found him attractive.

The fifty-two-year-old was a 1978 graduate of Indiana State University, and the classmate of its most famous alumni, Hall of Fame basketball player Larry Bird. Tommy was the second highest ranking administrator at the Indianapolis Medical Center, which was the largest hospital in the state of Indiana.

"Hello?" Tommy answered.

"Mr. Sanford, my name is Ray Schrader, and I'm calling from the Tucson Police Department here in Arizona. Do you have a minute or two to talk?"

"Sure, Officer, call me Tommy. What's this about?"

"Do you still own a set of Ping Eye 2 golf clubs?"

"Why do you ask?"

"We are working on a case, and one of the clubs from a set that we think you may have owned has now become part of the investigation. Do you still have them?"

"Not anymore, but I wish I did. I got new clubs about two years ago, and I don't hit them worth a darn. I sold the old ones on eBay."

"Is there any chance you would still have the record of who purchased the clubs?" Ray asked hopefully.

Tommy had never thrown any records away, no matter how insignificant. "I'm sure I have it somewhere. I won't be home for a few hours, where can I reach you?"

Ray gave Tommy his number and thanked him for his cooperation. He ended the call by indicating a sense of urgency: "I'm looking forward to your call."

Ray took a quick, refreshing, and reflective pause before sharing his accomplishments with his captain. He was unaware that in the next few minutes, the shit would hit the fan.

CHAPTER TWENTY-SIX

JEFF SCOTT'S FULL title was the national director of marketing and sales for Ping Golf. He accepted this position in 1995 after having served in the same capacity for eleven years with Titleist.

A handful of administrative assistants screened all of Jeff's calls, except for a very select few individuals, including Don Weber, who had access to his private line. Jeff and Don played golf collegiately at the University of Nebraska in the early seventies and remained close friends over the years. Don asked Jeff to be the godfather of his first child, Greg, and he was honored to do so.

The computer system at Ping Golf indicated the historical activity of all inquiries, repairs, and replacements of every set of clubs that Ping had ever sold. Ping guaranteed their clubs for life, provided that they were not damaged due to neglect. They kept this detailed record in the event that a hot-headed golfer, who snapped his wedge over his knee in anger, would try to get Ping to replace it three or four times a year.

When a second phone call came in that Monday asking about a Ping Eye 2, serial number 14684, this time from a police detective in California, an alert operator saw Jeff Scott's name on the previous inquiry and forwarded the call directly to his office.

The winter storm that was rampaging outside had intensified and now pounded the greater Phoenix area with dangerous cloud-to-ground lightning. Jeff questioned the wisdom of calling his friend in Tucson for fear that he would receive an electrical shock over the active phone line, but his sense of urgency trumped his concern for personal safety.

"Don, it's Jeff," he said as his friend could hear the thunder in the background. "Let me make this quick, all hell is breaking loose up here."

"Go ahead, Jeff, what is it?" asked Don.

"We just got a call up here asking about a Ping Eye 2 from a cop over in California, and it had the same serial number that you gave me this morning. What in God's name is going on?"

"It's a long story. Call me back when your weather breaks," answered Don, not wanting to leave his good friend in peril. "Just quickly give me the cop's name and number."

At the police station, Ray had just taken a few steps toward Mike office when the ringing of his phone stopped him dead in his tracks. He returned to his desk to answer the phone in hopes that the person on the other end of the line was Tommy Sanford, calling with another piece of the puzzle. "This is Officer Ray Schrader," he said, still having a difficult time referring to himself as a detective.

"Officer, this is Don Weber over here at Randolph."

Ray could feel the blood rushing to his head as Don repeated the message he had just received from his good friend Jeff Scott. Before he could finish writing down the California officer's name and number, his second line lit up, and he apologetically put Don on hold.

"This is Officer Ray Schrader," he repeated for the second time in less than a minute.

"This is Tommy Sanford calling, and I just got a call from a detective, Joshua Present, from out in California. He was asking me the same questions you were. I gave him your name and number, I hope that was OK."

Before Ray could answer, his third line now lit up, as he placed Tommy Sanford on hold along with Don Weber.

For a third time, a now puzzled and frazzled Ray Schrader punched line three. "Schrader!"

The voice on the other end was caught off guard by Ray's greeting. "This is Detective Josh Present with the Del Mar California Police Department."

Joshua Present's picture could easily have been on the cover of any Beach Boys album back in the late sixties. He learned to surf as a teenager and was still as blonde, tan, and fit as he had been in high school twenty years earlier. The San Diego State graduate still donned his wet suit twice a week, although now he spent more time teaching his twin fourteen-year-old daughters the graceful art of riding the waves. At work, he was casually yet impeccably dressed in a short sleeve shirt, tie, and color-coordinated cuffed khakis. On the weekends and after hours, you would normally find Josh wearing traditional surfer attire, baggies, and Huarachi sandals from the Beach Boys' classic song "Surf City". He had at one time considered a career in modeling, and even had appeared in a number of fashion magazines, but gave that up for what he felt was a more rewarding and challenging career in law enforcement. Josh was promoted to detective of the Del Mar Police Department in 2001, following the retirement of his predecessor.

Detective Present said, "I think we need to talk."

"We sure do!" Ray responded. "I've got a couple of guys on hold—let me get rid of them. Give me two shakes."

Ray put the detective on hold as he thanked Don for the heads up about Joshua Present but indicated that he had the California detective holding on another line.

After dismissing Don, Ray picked up his second line and said to Tommy Sanford, "I'm sorry for having you wait."

"That's OK. What in the hell is going on?"

"I don't know, but I'm about to find out. Listen, I've got that California detective on another line, so I need to get back to him, but call me when you find the name of the person who bought those Pings from you. I need that name!"

Tommy Sanford responded, "I'm on my way home right now. I'll try and find it. The California cop wants the name also."

"Give me the name, and I'll give it to him," said Ray, wanting to keep control of the investigation for the moment. "Save yourself the call."

Ray then thanked Tommy again before he picked up line three.

For the next few minutes, the two detectives shared the pieces of their puzzles that resulted in the crossing of their paths. Detective Joshua Present explained how the body of a soon-to-be identified man was found presumably beaten to death with a Ping Eye 2 five iron in the parking lot of the Del Mar Racetrack. The bloody weapon was left next to the body with the serial number 14684 plainly visible. Detective Present explained that he contacted Ping Golf, eventually spoke with Jeff Scott, and was given the name of Tommy Sanford along with the address of the Oakwood Country Club in Indianapolis, Indiana. After speaking with Oakwood's head pro, Rick Held, he had Sanford's cell number along with the knowledge that he was the second officer who had requested the exact same information in a matter of hours. He then called Tommy who reiterated his previous conversation with Officer Schrader and gave him Ray's number. Tommy had also promised Detective Present the name and address of the person who purchased his old clubs if he could find the paperwork. His phone call to Officer Ray Schrader now completed his serendipitous journey.

Ray then explained to Detective Present how the beaten body of Nick Trikilos was found in the lounge of the Randolph Golf Complex, beaten to death with a Ping Eye 2 seven iron with the same serial number involved in the Del Mar homicide. Ray didn't need to explain *his* investigative trail because Joshua Present had just taken it. He chose not to share any other information at that time, including the existence of a composite sketch of their suspect—Round Face Tony.

"At this point," said Ray, "I need to turn all of this over to my captain, Mike Groman, who is leading this investigation. Let me get him up to speed, then we'll have a conference call to discuss our next steps."

"That'll be fine, Ray, can I call you Ray?" asked Detective Present.

"Yeah, that's what everyone calls me. And what about you?"

"Josh is good. We're pretty informal here in southern California."

After jotting down Detective Present's phone number, Ray nervously made his way to Mike Groman's office to explain the bizarre twist the investigation had just taken.

CHAPTER TWENTY-SEVEN

THE CLOSED-DOOR MEETING between Mike and Ray lasted just a little over an hour. During that time, Mike called the chief of police with an update, Floyd was mercifully summoned back to the squad room, Tommy Sanford had not yet called with information about who purchased his clubs, and a fifty-plus mile per hour wind gust had temporarily knocked out the power, leaving the entire police station in the dark. When the emergency generators finally kicked in, the buzzing of rebooting computers could be heard up and down each hallway.

The apparent relationship between the murders of Nick Trikilos on Tuesday and the yet-to-be-identified victim from Del Mar on Friday had changed the course of the investigation. If Round Face Tony was indeed their prime suspect in both cases, his last known whereabouts was over three hundred miles to the west of Tucson.

"Let's get Del Mar on the phone," said Mike. Ray quickly passed the phone number of the California detective across the desk to his waiting captain.

"Detective Present, this is Mike Groman calling from Tucson."

After a short pause, Mike continued, "OK, Josh. Everyone here calls me Mike."

The fact that Mike and Josh abandoned their formal titles with no hesitation was recognition on both of their parts that this phone call was to be the first of many.

"Josh, I've got my two detectives here that are working this case with me, Floyd LeRud and of course you already know Ray Schrader. Do you mind if I put you on speaker?"

Before giving his permission, Josh responded, "That Ray did some nice police work." Although he was genuine in his praise of Ray, Josh realized that he inadvertently had praised himself at the same time.

Mike agreed with Josh, and then put the phone on speaker so that all three could be privy to the conversation.

"I'm really jealous of you guys," said Josh. "The Del Mar Police Department has a total of nine officers, and I'm the only detective."

"Well," Mike responded, "there are a lot of days when a small department like yours sounds pretty good."

"We haven't had a homicide here in Del Mar in over three years. That case was pretty straightforward—a jealous boyfriend shot his cheating girlfriend's lover. We had it wrapped up in a couple of days. Most of our time is spent with simple day to day stuff."

"So what do we know right now about your victim?" Mike asked, focusing the conversation back onto the investigation.

"Well, Mike, because we are so small, the San Diego County Sheriffs' Department's CSU is processing all of the evidence, and the county coroner is doing the autopsy. "I'm expecting both of those reports by tomorrow."

"Have you been able to ID the victim?"

"Not yet," answered Josh. "There was no wallet found at the scene. My first thought was that this was probably a mugging that went south, but now with your victim in Tucson, it's obvious that something else is going on."

"I'm sure you're right about that," Mike agreed.

"A short time ago," Josh continued, "we received a call from a Maria Cirillo, who had gone to Palm Springs on Friday to visit her sister. When she returned this morning, her husband Dominic was not at home. She told me that this was highly unusual because the two had planned on having brunch together when she got back. She called all of their friends and neighbors, but no one had seen him. When she found out about the homicide of a man at the Del Mar Racetrack, she panicked because her husband went there every Friday. One of her friends told her that the *Carmel Valley Tribune* gave a brief description of the victim, and while it sounded somewhat like Dominic, they reassured her that in all likelihood it was someone else."

"So where do we stand with her right now?" asked Mike.

"I told her that we normally wait twenty-four hours before investigating missing persons because the individual usually returns home with a simple explanation. But because of the circumstances surrounding this case, the coincidence that her husband was at the racetrack on Friday and that he matched the physical description of the victim, we ignored the twenty-four hour rule. She's at the morgue right now."

"How old of a guy was the victim?"

"If I had to guess, probably about seventy," answered Josh, "about the same age as Maria Cirillo. But I should warn you, I'm terrible at guessing people's ages. That and people's weights. I would never make it as a carnival worker."

In the spirit of cooperation, Josh offered, "When I get those reports tomorrow from the county, I'll fax over copies and call you as soon as we have a positive ID of the victim."

"Thanks, Josh." Mike realized it was now his turn to participate in the game of "if-you-show-me-yours-I'll-show-you-mine."

"As Ray probably already told you, we have the reports back from our CSU. I'll have him send you copies, but they're not much help. We also have a sketch of a possible suspect, who was the last known person seen with our victim, Nick Trikilos. We call our suspect Round Face Tony."

"You call him what?" asked a chuckling Josh Present.

"You heard me," Mike said. "When you see the picture, you'll understand. Our media ran it over the weekend, and one of my detectives spent the morning chasing his tail following up on a number of tips. I think it's obvious that Round Face Tony is long gone."

"Have you heard back from Tommy Sanford?"

"Not yet," Mike answered, "but we hope to shortly."

Mike and Josh then came to an agreement that there was no point in duplicating their efforts on this case. Since Mike Groman had more resources to devote to the investigation, Josh gladly relinquished the duty of following up with Tommy Sanford to the Tucson team. Both Josh and Mike realized that coordinating their efforts would benefit both investigations.

"We'll also send you everything we have on our victim Nick Trikilos," said Mike before bringing the conversation to a close.

"I'll do the same once we ID our victim," Josh responded. "I'm sure we will talk later today."

After hanging up the phone, Mike turned to Floyd and Ray, content with the new partnership he had just formed, and said, "It looks like we just opened up our Del Mar Substation!"

CHAPTER TWENTY-EIGHT

THE TWO-SQUARE-MILE CITY of Del Mar was founded by Theodore Loop, a worker for the Southern California Railroad Company. He and his wife Ella, who named the city after her favorite poem *The Fight on Paseo Del Mar*, began a tent city on the beach in 1882. They referred to the two-and-a-half-mile stretch of land as "the most beautiful place on the entire coast of California," and they may have been correct.

Del Mar sits on the northern edge of the Carmel Valley where the San Dieguito River, which flows from Lake Hodge to the east, meets the Pacific Ocean. Today, its forty-five hundred residents mostly work in downtown San Diego, which is a short twenty-minute commute on the *Coaster*. This train runs along the coastline twice an hour, originating in Oceanside in northern San Diego County and ending at the Santa Fe Station in the heart of downtown San Diego. The lifestyle in the sleepy ocean town of Del Mar is more relaxed and laid back than most areas of southern California.

The Del Mar Fairgrounds plays host to the annual San Diego County Fair, where the historic Del Mar Racetrack is its centerpiece. Unlike most fairgrounds, Del Mar bristles with activities all year round, hosting events from Cirque de Soleil to the Professional Bull Riders' Tour.

The seventy-two-year-old Dominic Cirillo shared a striking resemblance to the singer Tony Bennett, and on more than one occasion, he playfully used the mistaken identity to obtain seating at a crowded restaurant ahead of patrons who had reservations. A number of times, his scam was foiled by eager restaurant employees or patrons who would ask him to belt out a few lines of *I Left My Heart in San Francisco*. Unfortunately for Dominic, he was utterly unable to carry a tune. His matronly wife Maria enjoyed the attention that came with being in the company of a celebrity, albeit an impersonator.

Dominic Cirillo made an almost religious pilgrimage to the Del Mar Racetrack every Friday. During the horse-racing season, May through September, he loved to play the ponies and one time hit an exacta that paid him $8,900. During the off-season, the parking lot was transformed into an enormous farmers market where Dominic liked to pick up the freshest of ingredients for his legendary homemade marinara.

The San Diego County Coroners' autopsy showed that Mr. Cirillo was killed by one well-placed blow to the side of the head, directly over his right ear. He literally never knew what hit him, as the head of the club penetrated his skull.

The San Diego County CSU was unable to find any prints on the murder weapon, the Ping Eye 2 five iron, which was left laying next to the body of the victim. There were also no other useful clues. The contents of Dominic's large canvas shopping bag, which he brought from home to the track, were partially scattered about the parking lot. Along with numerous vine-ripened tomatoes, garlic, peppers, and onions, the victim was clutching in his right hand a single fresh red rose, which the seventy-two-year-old man would have placed in a vase on Maria's nightstand, exchanging it for the one he had purchased the previous Friday.

To identify the walletless victim, the San Diego County CSU took Dominic Cirillo's fingerprints and ran them through the national database.

They discovered that Dominic "Guy" Cirillo was the consigliere, or trusted advisor, to the Genovese Crime Family in New York from 1960 to 1968. At the age of thirty-two, he was sentenced to twenty-one years in prison, having been convicted on eighteen counts of conspiracy relating to gambling, drugs, prostitution, loan-sharking, and a protection racket. He was able to avoid the more serious charge of conspiracy to commit murder, which would have landed him a much longer sentence.

Dominic Cirillo was rewarded for his loyalty to the Genovese family, when he declined to turn informant for a reduced sentence, unlike the infamous Joseph Valachi, as described in his book *The Valachi Papers*. Upon his release from prison in 1985, which was four years early for good behavior, the financially secure forty-nine-year-old former mobster retired to southern California and kept his past life surreptitious.

His first and only wife, Maria, whom he met in 1991 at the age of fifty-five, believed he became a wealthy man upon selling his lucrative scrap metal business in New York. She knew nothing of his criminal, secretive past until Detective Joshua Present questioned her early Monday afternoon. Over the course of the past two days, her entire life had tragically fallen apart.

Back in Tucson, Detective Ray Schrader received the phone call from Tommy Sanford, who was able to locate the name and address of the person who had purchased his old set of Ping Eye 2s. In 2005, he had sold them to a Rodney Knapp in Scottsdale, Arizona, for $150.00, and shipped them via UPS on Friday, April 15—tax day.

Though still very windy, Monday's late afternoon sun cast long shadows as Mike answered his phone. "Mike Groman."

"Hi, Mike, this is Josh," Detective Present said with a degree of familiarity.

"Can you hang on a second while I get Floyd and Ray in here?" Mike asked almost rhetorically. With that, he summoned his two detectives with a frantic wave of his hand to get their attention.

"I'm going to put you on speaker again," said Mike, this time without requesting permission.

"Thanks for sending me all of your files on Nick Trikilos," said Josh, "I was just sitting down to start going through them."

"No problem, Josh. Any luck yet on your victim's ID?"

"It was Dominic Cirillo, Maria's husband, as we expected. She made the positive ID about three hours ago."

"Do we know anything about him?"

"I was expecting the autopsy and CSU folders tomorrow, but the courier dropped them off just a short time ago."

"So what do we know?"

Mike, Floyd, and Ray sat in an almost stunned silence as they listened to Josh Present relay the details of Dominic "Guy" Cirillo's life.

CHAPTER TWENTY-NINE

MOST OF MIKE Groman's conversations with the chief of police were conducted via telephone, and he could count on his one enormous hand the number of times that he had initiated the call. Chief George Sladek knew that there was something of critical importance when the captain of his homicide unit called and said, "George, it's Mike. I need to come up." If the mere fact of this phone call didn't indicate urgency, the tone of his voice did.

The passion that George Sladek had for his job could be easily seen in his steely blue eyes, reminiscent of Clint Eastwood's glint as Dirty Harry when he said, "Go ahead. Make my day." His permanently furled brow and crows feet revealed the toll that the eighteen stressful years he served as the chief of police had taken on him. George's detectable limp was the result of a bullet he took in 1984, with the grace of God being the only barrier between him and the life of a quadriplegic. To this day, the bullet remains lodged precariously close to his spinal chord, as doctors at that time determined its removal to be to risky.

George was seated behind his well-organized desk at 5:45 PM when Mike walked briskly past the secretary's recently vacated station and through the open door leading into the chief's office. George got up and made his captain feel welcomed by greeting him in the center of the room.

"It's good to see you again, Mike," he said, as he warmly shook his hand. "Please, have a seat," he continued, directing Mike to a pair of black leather upholstered chairs that faced his desk. "Can I offer you a drink?" the chief asked before sitting down. "You look like you could use one."

Because it was after hours and Mike was technically off the clock, he answered, "Scotch, neat, if you have it." He was well aware that his boss drank Dewers.

After pulling a bottle from his desk drawer, George poured two equal and more than generous portions into a couple of coffee mugs that he kept on a shelf behind his desk. The chances were pretty good that these two cups seldom held coffee.

Handing Mike his drink, George took a seat next to him in the other black leather chair, making it a point to never use his desk as a barrier to separate himself from his guest. If there were multiple visitors, chairs would be added to form either a triangle, square, or circle.

"So this is about the Nick Trikilos case, isn't it?"

"We've got a real cluster fuck on our hands," Mike answered. For the next forty-five minutes, Mike went over every minute detail of the case with the chief, leaving absolutely nothing out.

"If we have one more body, we'll be investigating a mass murder," Mike concluded. "With the possible mob connection, who knows what we're looking at?"

"What do you want to do?" asked George.

Mike knew that George's question was meant to open the discussion into a consideration of whether the Tucson Police should turn the case over to the FBI or the Justice Department. Not one to ever back down from a challenge, Mike answered, "This is our case. Nick Trikilos was murdered in *our* city."

"That's the right goddamn answer!" exclaimed a supportive George Sladek as he grabbed Mike's now-empty mug, adding, "Let me freshen that up for you."

As Chief Sladek made his way to his desk, Mike said, "Go easy, George, I've got to make it home tonight."

"What do you need from me?" George asked, while pouring two more drinks.

"The first thing I needed, you just gave me," answered Mike, referring to George's support of his desire to retain jurisdiction over the case and not the scotch.

"What else?" continued George, who had returned to his chair.

"I might need some travel vouchers at some point."

"Done. What else?"

"Man power wise, I'm all set with the two officers you gave me, and tomorrow I'm going to make Dave Starbuck the acting captain. I need to be working this case full time."

"How are those two working out? What are their names again?" asked George.

"Floyd LeRud and Ray Schrader. They're very good," answered Mike. "Both of them are hard workers with good instincts. They're keepers."

"That's good to hear. Listen, Mike, you know our budget is tight, but we are not going to try to do this on the cheap. This is high priority for me. Do you understand what I am saying?"

"I sure do, George, and thanks."

George ended the meeting by taking Mike's now-empty coffee cup, shaking hands and saying, "Keep me informed and don't lose your receipts. We don't want to drive the bean counters crazy."

It was now dark outside, as the sun had set around 6:00 PM. The howling winds, that had earlier in the day messed up Mike's hair and interrupted the power to the police station, had now diminished. As Mike made his way to his car, his mind was racing.

His first thought focused on his ability to safely operate his vehicle, considering the amount of scotch that was now in his system. Mike knew that he was definitely over the legal limit of .08 percent, but he had taken his chances before and always made it home without incident.

His second thought went back to the meeting he had just completed with George Sladek. On one hand, he was appreciative and honored that his boss had placed such an enormous amount of faith in him, while at the same time, he also began feeling the anxiety that accompanies great expectations.

His third thought went to his young detectives, Floyd and Ray, as he wondered if they were truly up to the challenges that lay ahead.

His fourth and final thought was of his wife, Jeanie, who was at her monthly mah-jongg game and not at home preparing his dinner. Claiming to be unable to boil water or pour cold milk over cereal, Mike stopped at his favorite fast food restaurant, Sonic, and ordered two cheeseburgers, sans onion and mayo, a large order of tater tots, and an extra thick chocolate milkshake to go.

Mike successfully made it home without incident at 9:45 PM, only moments before Jeanie walked in the door. He ate his dinner while watching the ten o'clock news, which now reported a possible connection between the homicide of Nick Trikilos in Tucson and another in southern California. Mike tossed and turned long after his 11:00 PM bedtime, thinking about the two murder victims and Round Face Tony.

CHAPTER THIRTY

B Y TUESDAY MORNING, Mike's adrenaline had more than made up for his restless night of sleep. His reorganizational meeting with his five regular detectives, Dave Starbuck, Sandra Lara, Jeff Green, Bob Stewart, and Steve Kraus, along with Floyd and Ray, had begun promptly at 8:00 AM. He explained how the recent developments in the Trikilos case would now require his full attention. As a result, he needed to temporarily abdicate his position as captain and place his second in command, Dave Starbuck, into the position of *acting captain*, a familiar role he had filled during Mike's numerous replacement surgeries.

Dave, a more than capable substitute and an excellent detective, would never be promoted to captain because he lacked the necessary managerial skills, and more importantly, an interest in the position. Unlike his previous tours of duty, this one would be of an indeterminate length.

"Dave has run this shop before," Mike said, as he concluded the meeting. "I'm sure we won't miss a beat. I'll still be around if you need my help."

Mike then gestured to Floyd and Ray to remain seated as he dismissed the others.

On the drive into work that morning, Mike debated with himself whether he would share with Floyd and Ray the contents of his meeting with the chief of police the previous evening. On one hand, he wanted them to know that the three of them had the chief's complete and total support. But on the other, he feared his two new detectives would feel unnecessary pressure knowing that the chief had a close eye on their investigation. In the end, Mike chose not to discuss the conversation he had the previous evening. Feeling pressure, whether produced internally or received externally, came with the territory for any detective that was worth his salt. Mike feared, however, that exposing his two young detectives to an excessive amount could interfere with their ability to perform at the high level that they had demonstrated up to this point.

"Are you guys ready to get to work?" Mike asked rhetorically, indicating a subtle and more serious approach to the investigation.

Their first order of business involved taking two of the large, unused white boards from the squad room and moving them into Mike's office. Although Dave Starbuck was the acting captain, the transfer of power was only temporary, so Mike maintained the lease on his space. Each of the three grabbed an erasable marker and began reconstructing a time line of the events of the past week, complete with names, dates, and phone numbers of each individual involved. After numerous edits, the trio eventually agreed upon the finished product. They also left a fair amount of space for future additions. Mike was a visual learner, and for him, the information now presented on the white board in this format was a tremendous aid.

Using the newly created board as a reference, Mike began passing out assignments.

"Floyd, get in touch with Jeff Scott at Ping Golf. Tell him that if there are any more calls asking about our set of Ping Eye 2 golf clubs, I'm the first goddamn one to know about it. Give him my cell number."

Now turning to Ray, Mike said, "Find me a phone number for Rodney Knapp up in Scottsdale. He may have gotten those clubs from Tommy Sanford, but I can guarantee that Mr. Knapp is not Round Face Tony *either*," implying that at one time Tommy had also been a suspect. "We're going to follow the golf club trail as far as we can."

Now that he had an empty office for the first time that Tuesday morning, Mike closed his door for privacy and called the two people who had spent over four hours golfing with Round Face Tony: Steve Brennan and Mark Schenck.

Mike was surprised when Mark answered the phone, as he was told that his jury duty would last until at least Wednesday. Mark Schenck explained that an eleventh hour plea agreement had been reached and that the jury was subsequently dismissed with the appreciation of the court. Mark accepted Mike's invitation to meet at Jerry-Bobs Restaurant in a half an hour for coffee and a few more questions.

Steve Brennan, likewise, told Mike that he had no trouble attending the meeting.

Occasionally, Mike Groman liked to conduct group interviews. He believed that each witness could help the others recall suppressed details or events. Additionally, Mike felt that this pair, having had a few days to reflect, might possibly have more information to offer as is sometimes the case after a short passage of time.

Floyd and Ray returned to Mike's office after completing their simple tasks. Ray handed his captain the phone number for Rodney Knapp, which he simply found in the Scottsdale phone directory.

"Mr. Knapp, this is Captain Mike Groman with the Tucson Police Department," Mike began.

Mike explained to Rodney the circumstances leading to his phone call. As luck would have it, Rodney Knapp was a manufacturer's representative for a large plumbing supplier and was about to make his weekly trip to Tucson. The two agreed to meet at the police station at 11:30 AM, following Rodney's earlier appointment with a customer. This timeframe fit in perfectly with Mike's prior engagement at Jerry-Bobs.

Mike, Floyd, and Ray arrived at the restaurant at 9:25 AM, five minutes prior to their scheduled meeting with Steve Brennan and Mark Schenck, who were each running a bit late. Today was much different than their previous visit to Jerry-Bobs when they almost had the entire place to themselves. Although the three detectives didn't have to wait for a table, there was only one available, which they immediately grabbed. The loud banging of dishes by the busboys forced the patrons to speak in raised voices, while nine waitresses scurried about, tending to their flock. It was clear to Mike, Floyd, and Ray that this place was controlled bedlam. Within the next fifteen minutes, however, there would be a mass exodus by the customers, who seemed to finish their breakfasts almost simultaneously, and would dash for the doors in the same way cockroaches react to sudden light.

After their coffee arrived, Mike briefly prepared his two detectives for the upcoming interview. "When we talk to Steve and Mark, don't be afraid to jump in. We're all in this thing together."

Sometimes, just a few simple words can speak volumes. Whether it was intentional or not, Captain Mike Groman had just anointed Floyd and Ray as official members of the team, with the magnitude of his statement hitting each like a twelve-pound sledge.

Steve Brennan arrived a few minutes before Mark Schenck, and each apologized for being late. Having not seen each other since their golf outing exactly one week ago, both Steve and Mark agreed that is was a pleasure seeing each other again.

As the waitress poured coffees for the two newcomers, Mike began to fill Steve and Mark in about the progress of the case, although he decided to leave out some of the more important details of the investigation. "We're kind of at a dead end right now, and we thought that if we talked again you might be able to remember something that could help us."

Steve, answering for both Mark and himself, said, "We'll do the best we can."

Mike explained that since their previous meeting, he had checked their story and started putting together the rudimentary pieces of the puzzle. He told Steve and Mark that he had narrowed the scope of the investigation down to one individual, Round Face Tony. He wanted them to focus on this mysterious individual.

Floyd, taking Mike at his word, jumped in and asked one of the first questions. "When you came down to the police station last Friday and worked with Officer Walker on the composite sketch," refreshing their memories, "we were only interested in what Tony looked like. Today, let's talk about what he said and how he acted. Did anything about him seem odd or out of the ordinary?"

"Good question," Mike thought to himself.

"I was riding in the cart with Nick, so I didn't have as much to do with him as Mark did," Steve answered, as a somber look crossed his face as he mentally memorialized his good friend.

Now on the spot, Mark said, "I do remember a couple of things I thought at the time were a little bit odd."

"Like what?" asked Mike.

"Well, the second hole at Dell Urich is a short par three with a lake to the left. He hit his tee shot into the sand bunker in front of the green. His second shot landed softly on the green with a lot of backspin and stopped just four feet from the hole. It was a really good shot."

When Mark paused to take a sip of coffee, Floyd asked, "What's unusual about that?"

"Let me finish. Then, as is customary, he raked the bunker to leave it smooth for the next golfer that might land in it. Then he raked and raked and raked some more." Then Mark joked, "He might still be there if we hadn't said something."

"God, he did take forever," recalled Steve. "Nick made some smart ass comment to him, like 'let's hurry up, my suit is going out of style.'"

Mark finished this story by adding, "He was in a couple of more bunkers, but we nipped that in the bud by saying something to him before he began raking."

Steve then recalled another peculiarity. "Another thing he did that was strange was that after each shot, he would use his golf towel to meticulously clean the club."

Because Mike was not a golfer, he asked, "Is that unusual?"

Steve answered, "Unless it happens to be muddy, most golfers clean their clubs at the end of the round. Last Tuesday, the course was very dry."

The conversation then evolved to the suspect's clubs. Mark said, "His clubs were a very old set of Pings, and I'd never seen that model before. His set also included a one and two iron that no one uses anymore. Those clubs are really hard to hit. I don't know how he did it, but he used that one iron a couple of times and hit the hell out of it."

Steve confirmed Mark's story. "Yeah, he outdrove all of us by thirty yards on the tenth hole, remember, Mark?"

Reminiscing, Mark answered, "I sure do, he took it down the right side," then admiringly added, "with a little draw."

"Draw?" Mike asked.

"Oh," Mark said, as he recalled he was speaking with a nongolfer, "that's when your golf shot gently curves from right to left because you put some spin on the ball. It's a pretty desired shot. You get a lot of roll for extra distance."

After a brief pause and sensing the conversation was losing momentum, Mike asked, "What did you guys talk about?"

"Not much," answered Mark. "We mostly talked about golf and told some jokes, though I did most of the talking."

"I did ask him what kind of work he did," added Steve. "He said that he owned an exterminating business back in New York. I assumed from that he was a snowbird."

Ray, who to this point had been uninvolved in the conversation, began asking a series of seemingly bizarre questions that the others took as a sign of his inexperience. "Did Round Face Tony laugh at the jokes?"

Mark answered, "Not as hard as I did, especially the one about the priest, the rabbi, and Raquel Welch."

Steve chimed in, "That was one of Nick's favorites. I must have heard it thirty times, but the way he told it, I laughed every time."

Mike and Floyd were hoping for a replay of the joke, but Ray remained intent on his line of questioning. "Do you think he *understood* the joke?"

Neither Steve nor Mark knew quite how to answer this question, while Mike and Floyd looked on with puzzled faces.

"Let me ask you this," Ray jumped in without permitting Steve or Mark to respond to his initial query. "Did Round Face Tony initiate conversation or just respond? Was he overly polite and well mannered? Was his speech casual or formal?"

Steve and Mark needed some time to ponder these questions. After recollecting the mannerisms of their strange golfing partner, they came to the conclusion that Round Face Tony was indeed overly polite and that his responses were unusually proper.

Ray's questions seemingly killed the interview, although the detectives were confident that they obtained everything the witnesses had to offer.

Now aware that his main suspect may not have been the easiest person to engage in conversation, Mike asked Steve, "So how did Nick talk to this guy for a couple of hours after the two of you left?" Mike didn't necessarily expect Steve to have an answer.

"You had to know Nick," Steve replied. "He loved to hear himself talk and tell stories—more so when he was drinking."

Shortly thereafter, their interview came to an end. Mike picked up the check, Steve Brennan headed back to Fitz, while Mark Schenck stopped at the Safeway grocery store to pick up some steaks for dinner before making his way home.

The three detectives made their way out into the parking lot and to their police car for their trip back to the station. Mike's attention was now on Ray Schrader and his peculiar questions which he seemingly had the answers to in advance.

CHAPTER THIRTY-ONE

"MY MOTHER IS a special education teacher, and she first suspected my brother Eddie was autistic when he was about four months old," said Ray on his trip back to the station with Mike and Floyd.

Ray went on to briefly describe his brother's classic early symptoms. "When Eddie was an infant, my mom suspected that something was wrong with him when he was unable to smile at people, follow moving objects, respond to loud noises, babble, and grasp and hold objects—simple stuff that normal babies do. By the age of two, the diagnosis was confirmed when he hadn't learned to walk, used no more than a few words, couldn't push a toy, or understand the function of household items."

After a brief pause, Ray added, "Steve Brennan and Mark Schenck could have been describing my twenty-year-old brother Eddie."

"So you're saying that Round Face Tony is autistic?" asked Mike.

"I guarantee it," Ray answered confidently. "And I'd bet that he is also obsessive compulsive."

"Like Jack Nicholson in that movie, oh, what was the name of it?" asked Floyd.

"*As Good as it Gets*," answered Ray, "with Helen Hunt."

"That's it!" Floyd said, confirming Ray's recollection.

"The excessive raking of the bunker and the cleaning of the clubs would be typical behaviors of someone with obsessive compulsive disorder."

Mike was skeptical. "I know about OCD, but isn't autism kind of like mental retardation?"

"Not even close," answered Ray. "In fact, people with autism tend to be highly intelligent, if not gifted, particularly in the areas of music and math. There are various levels of autism, and my guess is that Round Face Tony, like my brother, has a mild form of the disorder. The politeness, the formal speech, and not understanding jokes are classic signs of mild adult autism."

"So getting back to that intelligence thing," Mike asked, "are you saying that Round Face Tony may be smarter than us?"

"No offense, Captain," Ray chuckled, "but I could almost guarantee it!"

Back at the station, and with about forty-five minutes before the expected arrival of Rodney Knapp, Mike Groman called Josh Present in Del Mar, California, to check on the progress of his case. "Good morning, Josh, this is Mike in Tucson. I'm on with Floyd and Ray."

"Hi, guys. I was just getting ready to give you a call."

"So what's going on at your end?"

Getting right to the point, Josh said, "The *Carmel Valley Tribune* ran the composite of Round Face Tony in this morning's edition." He now understood, after seeing the sketch, why Mike and his team had labeled their suspect Round Face.

"I might have something here," he continued.

Along the Pacific Coast Highway, there are a number of small mom-and-pop motels, many of which were built before the construction of the interstate. Most of them are quite charming and have quaint names like the Wave Runner and the Water's Edge, which reflect their close proximity to the ocean.

"The manager of the Seaside Motel saw his picture and claims our boy stayed there Thursday and Friday nights and checked out early Saturday morning. I'm here with her right now," explained Josh. "Just like your witnesses, she guessed that he was in his mid to late fifties, five-feet-ten-inches tall, and about two hundred pounds."

"What else do we know?" asked Mike.

"According to the information on his registration form, his name is Tony Bianco from Scottsdale, Arizona."

Mike interrupted, sensing there was going to be a fair amount of information. "Slow down, Josh, let me get this down." Mike opened his note pad and began scribbling notes, as Ray and Floyd, taking the cue from their captain, did the same. "Is that B-I-A-N-C-O?"

"That's right," answered Josh. "It says on his motel registration form that he is from Scottsdale, Arizona. He gives his address as 1331 Calle Ocotillo and a home phone number of 885-0033. He didn't put an area code. The only other information is his license plate number ADF 1287 on a black 2006 Lincoln Town Car."

"Did he pay with a credit card?" Mike interrupted, but then immediately felt embarrassed that he had just treated Josh Present like a rookie detective, as Josh would have undoubtedly given him this important information if it was available.

However, Josh, who either ignored the slight or was unaware of it, told Mike the manager's story of how their suspect paid with cash, which happened to be a violation of the motel's policy that mandated the use of a credit card. As with most hotels and motels, the Seaside Motel required its guests to pay with plastic so that in the event there was any damage to the room, the motel would have some recourse. Round Face Tony claimed that he had lost his wallet on the beach, and that his brother had wired him money, enough for a motel room, food, and gas for his trip back to Arizona on Saturday. Because Round Face Tony seemed like a very nice man and because business just happened to be slow that day, the manager felt sorry for him and bent their rules.

"Ask her if the guy was extremely polite," said Mike.

"Ask her what?" replied Josh, not certain that he had heard his Tucson counterpart correctly.

"Ask her if our guy was maybe the most polite and courteous person she had ever met."

"Hang on, I'll ask her," said Josh.

After a short pause, Josh got back on the line. "How did you know?"

Mike explained his team's autism and OCD theory, which made perfect sense to Josh.

"I just called the CSU to process his room," Josh said as he changed the subject. "No one has used his room since he checked out on Saturday, though the maid had already cleaned. They should be here any minute now," finished Josh.

"Good thinking," said Mike. "How long will it take to get their report back?"

"Well, since it's only Tuesday, probably by Thursday at the earliest, depending on their case loads," answered Josh. "Hopefully this time they will find something that's more useful than what they were able to find at Dominic Cirillo's murder scene."

"I'll run a background check on Tony Bianco," offered Mike.

"That'll be great. Call me when you know something."

Looking skeptically at the scant information that Josh Present was able to provide about Tony Bianco, Mike handed his notes to Floyd and Ray, and then asked them to run the check.

Of the seven male Biancos living in the greater Phoenix area, none were named Tony or Anthony. Additionally, the photos of each provided by the DMV looked nothing like their suspect. They returned to Mike Groman's office after about twenty minutes and delivered the disappointing news that he had expected.

"There is no such address, not even a street named Calle Ocotillo, and according to the phone company, the phone number is nonexistent. The DMV says the same for the license plate," reported Floyd.

"I knew it was too good to be true," said Mike. "Would you guys call Josh and break the news?"

A few moments later, Rodney Knapp arrived at the Tucson Police Station. It was hard to believe that anyone could dwarf Mike Groman, but Rodney Knapp could claim that unique distinction. At six-feet-eight-inches tall and 340 pounds, Rodney was a hulk of a man who outsized the captain by two inches and fifty-five pounds. Mike felt uncomfortable being in the unaccustomed position of looking up to someone of a greater stature.

"You must have played some football," Mike said to the much younger behemoth.

"I was an Arizona State Sun Devil," Rodney answered. "I played ball back in the mideighties for Coach Coop."

"How was the ride down?"

This was a typical question that anyone would have asked of a person who had just made the drive from Phoenix to Tucson. Interstate 10, which connects the two cities, may be the most treacherous eighty miles of highway in the United States. It consists of only two lanes headed in each direction, which was adequate for the traffic flow until the midseventies, when the enormous growth of both cities and the increased traffic rendered this stretch of highway impotent. The state has been desperately trying to add an extra lane in each direction, but the construction zones only add to the congestion problems and will continue to do so for at least the next decade. Accidents and rollovers are common occurrences and often leave the highway closed for hours, as victims are airlifted to the nearest medical facility. The only reprieve from the boring stretch of highway is found at the halfway point between Tucson and Phoenix, where Picacho Peak juts high into the Arizona sky. This was the site of the furthest western battle of the Civil War, which is playfully reenacted each spring.

"The drive down was uneventful," answered Rodney.

Mike then got down to business by asking Rodney about the purchase of his Ping Eye 2s from Tommy Sanford.

"A buddy of mine who plays golf wanted me to take up the game," said Rodney. "I knew virtually nothing about the game, but my friend suggested Pings when I went to buy my clubs. I found out that a new set would cost about a thousand dollars, so I went on eBay and found a set for $150.00. I figured it was a good deal. I had the clubs for only about a month and played a number of times, but I hated the game. After I decided to give up golf, I took out an ad in the *Arizona Republic* and got most of my money back."

"Can you tell us about the guy who bought them from you?" asked Mike.

"Sure," answered Rodney. "He called me on the first day my ad appeared in the paper."

"Do you remember what the ad said?" asked Floyd.

"It was real simple," Rodney answered. "I didn't want to spend too much, you know, sending good money after bad. All it said was Ping Eye 2 irons, full set 1 to 9, P plus S, $125.00 and then my phone number."

"Can you remember what he said when he called?" asked Mike.

"Not exactly, but talking to him on the phone, something told me that he was some kind of nut case."

"Why was that?" asked Mike.

"He kept asking me over and over again about the numbers on the clubs. For some reason, the set of numbers one through nine was real important to him. He had to have those nine clubs. He didn't seem that interested in the two wedges."

"Would you recognize him again if you saw him?" asked Floyd.

"I'm pretty sure," Rodney answered. "He was kind of an odd-looking guy with dark hair and a full face."

Floyd knew that showing the sketch of Round Face Tony to Rodney would be a mere formality, but he did so nonetheless. Rodney confirmed its likeness.

"Can you remember anything else about him?" Mike asked.

"I thought it was odd that the guy paid the full price and didn't try to negotiate a better deal as people normally do with this type of sale. I also remember that he paid with three brand new fifty-dollar bills that stuck together. After I gave him his change, he thanked me again and again for selling him the clubs."

With nothing further to discuss, the three detectives escorted Rodney Knapp from the police station. On their way out, Ray asked if he could recall anything about the car that Round Face Tony had driven to his house that day.

Rodney answered, "It was full sized, maybe a Lincoln or a Cadillac, and dark, possibly black."

It was now a few minutes past noon. Mike graciously treated his two detectives to lunch at Chuy's, one of Mike's favorite and inexpensive Mexican restaurants. Upon their return to the office, the three detectives would spend the remainder of the day working on their *tens*, which were case reports that were typed on the Tucson Police Department's form 1010, and hence the shorthand nickname.

CHAPTER THIRTY-TWO

I NEVER MUCH liked the desert. Some do and some don't. I grew up in New York, but moved out west with my father and three brothers almost thirty years ago. Westchester County was so green, while everything here is a sandy brown.

This area, on the outskirts of Henderson, Nevada, is particularly barren. Why John Smallwood chose to reside here is beyond me. Judging from his opulent estate, it is obvious that he could have afforded to live anywhere, but instead he chose 230 Crooked Tree Lane.

Finding the whereabouts of my third victim, like Nick Trikilos and Dominic Cirillo before him, would have been much more difficult just ten years ago. The Internet, along with the expansion of the Freedom of Information Act back in the midnineties, allowed me to locate these individuals with very little difficulty.

John Smallwood had a four o'clock appointment with his chiropractor every Tuesday afternoon. It would only take him about fifteen minutes to drive to his doctor's office, although he always left about a half an hour early. This day was no exception.

I pulled my car off onto the gravel shoulder of Crooked Tree Lane at 3:15. I then popped the hood of my car, slightly loosened a battery cable, and then stood along side my vehicle as though I was having a mechanical problem. I was counting on John Smallwood to stop and offer assistance. He did exactly what I had hoped.

From where I had parked, I could look down the road toward Highway 93, with an unobstructed view for almost a mile. I could do the same in the other direction, back toward the Smallwood estate. Except for his approaching Mercedes, no other cars were visible in either direction on this desolate road. All I needed to do was to get him out of his car.

"Do you need some help?" asked John Smallwood, as he stopped his car along side of mine and rolled down the passenger side window.

"Thanks for stopping," I replied. "I think I have a bad battery. Could you give me a jump?"

"I've got jumper cables in my trunk," he answered, before I had the chance to tell him that I had them as well. "Let me pull around and see what we can do."

He maneuvered his Mercedes so that our cars were then facing each other. He stepped out and walked to his trunk and reached in to grab his jumper cables. When he stood up, I was all over him with my two iron.

Unlike Dominic Cirillo, who never saw the attack coming, this victim offered some resistance. He blocked my first number of swings with his arms and hands, and then dropped to the ground in only what could be described as a defensive fetal position. Getting a clear shot at his head was difficult, as he was instinctively protecting it with his arms and hands. I began whacking his body indiscriminately until he eventually dropped his arms, at which point I was able to finish him off.

I don't understand why, but I scooped up his lifeless body and deposited him into the trunk of his car. I left the two iron resting against his fender.

I was exhausted and out of breath as I looked around and saw no one coming in either direction. I noticed that my shirt and pants were splattered with blood, and I desperately needed clean clothing. I went to the trunk of my car, opened my suitcase, and then changed right in the middle of Crooked Tree Lane. I can't stand dirty, let alone blood stained clothing.

I then went around to the front of my car, tightened my battery cable, closed the hood of my car, and drove off. I kept looking at John Smallwood's Mercedes in my rear view mirror until I reached Highway 93 and headed east toward the Hoover Dam.

Now, there's only one more to go.

CHAPTER THIRTY-THREE

JOHN SMALLWOOD GRADUATED from Harvard Law School in 1969 and finished in the top five percent of his class. He returned to his roots in New York City where he was hired as the second lawyer in a two-man office that he shared with Nathan Kuehner, who preceded him at Harvard just four years earlier.

The two young lawyers made a dynamic team, and within a few short years, their partnership began to grow exponentially. Over the next twenty years, they moved office space seven times, each time into larger quarters, and eventually settled on the top three floors of the prestigious midtown Goldwater Building. By this time, the law firm of Smallwood & Kuehner added eight additional full partners, over one hundred associates, and three hundred secretaries, paralegals, private investigators, and assorted technical specialists. If Smallwoood & Kuehner was not the highest grossing New York City law firm, it would definitely give the number one law firm a run for its money in the coming years.

At the January 2005 meeting of the senior partners, John Smallwood announced his retirement, which sent shock waves throughout the firm. At sixty-two years of age, he was still the firm's top litigator, having assumed the role after the retirement of Nathan Kuehner three years earlier. Instead of having multiple names on the letterhead, the law firm of Smallwood & Kuehner remains to this day, successfully continuing its founders' legacy.

John Smallwood's sudden announcement came after months of personal deliberation. His wife, MaryAnne, suffered from acute rheumatoid arthritis and needed to move to a drier climate. The Smallwoods' only offspring, Marshall, an orthopedic surgeon at the Las Vegas Medical Center, moved to Sin City in 1999 with his wife and two young children. Their encouragement made John and MaryAnne's decision of where to move a no-brainer, and the two settled in nearby Henderson in the summer of 2005.

While MaryAnne's affliction was arthritis, John suffered from a chronic bad back, undoubtedly exacerbated by years of inactivity and carrying an unnecessary forty extra pounds, which had settled around his waist.

When notified that John had failed to show for his weekly 4:00 PM adjustment at his chiropractor's office, MaryAnne instinctively knew that something was terribly wrong. John had never missed a chiropractic appointment in two years. The police found John Smallwood's 2008 Mercedes S600 parked along the north side of Crooked Tree Lane, which is a secluded three-mile stretch of road that leads from the Smallwood's twenty-acre desert estate to Highway 93. John's bludgeoned body was dumped in the trunk of his Mercedes, while a bloody Ping Eye 2 two iron was propped up against the right rear fender.

By 5:30 PM on Tuesday, MaryAnne Smallwood had received the tragic news, while the Clark County CSU had set up floodlights at the crime scene and would be gathering evidence until well after midnight.

It was now Wednesday morning, exactly one week since Mike Groman was awakened from a sound sleep and summoned to the Randolph Golf Complex. Badge 803 and 119, Floyd LeRud and Ray Schrader, had enjoyed their temporary assignment to the homicide unit and were not looking forward to their inevitable return to their former positions as patrolmen. Sandy, Pete, Donna, and Don at the golf course had settled back into their daily routines. Sandy, however, continued to have nightmarish flashbacks of her discovery each morning as she made her way up the dimly lit path to open the Bar. Josh Present, the Del Mar detective, would spend the day following up on a number of possible Round Face Tony sightings and awaiting his CSU report, which would hopefully arrive the next day.

Mike was half listening to Muddy Waters on the radio while driving to work, as his mind was preoccupied with the details of this case. Although their suspect didn't match any of the seven Biancos provided by the DMV, he debated the wisdom of interviewing them nonetheless. On one hand, Round Face Tony might be a relative of one or more of these Biancos, and it's possible that one of them might be able to make a positive identification. On the other hand, if their suspect was smart enough to give the motel manager a bogus address, as well as phone and license plate numbers, why would he use his actual name or the name of someone who could identify him?

Before Mike came to a decision, his cell phone rang and the caller ID indicated it was Jeff Scott from Ping Golf. Mike knew there would only be one reason for him to call, and it would not be good news.

"This is Captain Groman."

"Captain, this is Jeff Scott with Ping Golf. I was told to give you a call if anyone else asked about your Ping Eye 2s."

After listening for a few moments, Mike said, "You've got to be shitting me. I'm driving into work right now. Can I call you back when I get to my office?"

CHAPTER THIRTY-FOUR

"COME ON IN, guys," Mike said to Ray and Floyd, as he walked past their desks. "We've got another goddamn victim."

Once all three had taken their seats inside Mike's office, the captain filled his two detectives in on the details of his brief conversation with Jeff Scott at Ping.

Jeff Scott had told Mike that a detective with the Clark County Sheriffs' Department had called to inquire about their specific Ping Eye 2 golf clubs. Because Jeff had been running late and was not in the office at the time of the call, his secretary had taken the message and delivered it to him immediately upon his arrival. Instead of talking with the Nevada detective, Jeff decided to pass the information directly on to Mike in an attempt to put an end to his current and hopefully final involvement in this case. Unable to write while he was driving, Mike arranged to call back once he was settled in his office to get the details.

"Mr. Scott, this is Captain Groman. Is this a good time?" Mike asked, although he didn't really care if the timing was good, bad, or otherwise for Jeff.

Mike's end of the conversation was very brief, as he mostly jotted down notes.

After hanging up with Jeff, Mike turned to Ray. "Put this name on the white board. It's Gary Stehlik, that's S-T-E-H-L-I-K." He then gave Ray the phone number.

Wasting no time at all, Mike called the Clark County detective and after a brief initial explanation of the purpose of his call, placed Detective Stehlik on speaker phone. Mike Groman and Gary Stehlik spent the next half hour sharing their information. The bottom line, however, was the fact that there were now three apparently related victims: John Smallwood, a recently retired New York City attorney, Dominic Cirillo, the former consigliere to the Genovese crime family, and Nick Trikilos, a saint with a suspected sordid and checkered past.

"I think what we need to do," suggested Gary, "is get in touch with John Smallwood's law firm and see if a former client has an ax to grind."

"That sounds good to me. Just getting a list of names shouldn't fall under their attorney/client privilege bullshit," Mike said, indicating a certain amount of disdain for lawyers.

"Listen, Mike, we have a resource here that might be a help to us that you don't have."

Curiously, Mike asked, "What's that?"

Detective Stehlik went on to describe the Nevada Gaming Commission, a regulatory government agency that oversees all aspects of gambling activities throughout the state.

"Back in the day," Gary said, "the first Las Vegas casinos were built and developed with organized crime money. In the early sixties, Robert Kennedy and the Justice Department began driving all of the hoodlums out of the gaming business. Today, the casinos are strictly regulated. Because the Justice Department is determined to make certain that organized crime does not slither back in, every casino employee must submit to a background check as a condition of employment. The investigative arm of the Nevada Gaming Commission has undoubtedly the most sophisticated computerized database of every organized crime group and individual, past or present, along with their entire genealogical family tree. The gaming commission shares the same system with United States Justice Department."

Gary then finished, "If anyone has even the slightest tie to organized crime, the system will spit them out."

"You're right, that's big time," Mike agreed, seeing the obvious benefits of that information.

"I wish you guys could come up," said Gary Stehlik. "It seems like we could sure help each other much easier if you were here."

Mike took the invitation as sincere. "My chief has given me the green light on this case, so give me an hour and let me see what I can do."

"That would be great," Gary said hopefully. "In the meantime, I'll call New York and see what Smallwood's law firm can give me."

After hanging up, Mike asked Floyd and Ray, "When was the last time you went to Vegas?" Each were surprised that Mike would include them in this facet of the investigation.

After giving Police Chief George Sladek an update, Mike secured three seats on Southwest Airlines flight 1406, which departed the Tucson International Airport at 1:20 PM. He also informed Gary Stehlik of their travel plans, who made arrangements to pick the trio up at Las Vegas McCarran International Airport. Gary also provided the Tucson team the use of a county vehicle, eliminating their need of a rental.

Meanwhile, Floyd had contacted Detective Josh Present in Del Mar and filled him in on the latest developments. On the directive of Mike Groman, he extended the invitation for Josh to join them in Las Vegas, but Josh had to regretfully decline. "My chief is not as generous as yours," Josh lamented. "Please keep me up to speed."

Mike, Floyd, and Ray raced home to pack. They agreed to meet back at the station by 11:30 AM, which would leave them enough time for lunch at Sonic before heading to the airport for their trip to Las Vegas.

CHAPTER THIRTY-FIVE

FROM GATE TO gate, Southwest Airlines flight 1406 from Tucson to Las Vegas lasted exactly one hour. The 132 passengers aboard passed from the Mountain to the Pacific time zone, which caused them to experience a time warp-like sensation, as their Tucson departure and Las Vegas arrival both occurred promptly at 1:20 PM.

The extremely busy McCarran International Airport handles the majority of the departing and arriving flights for forty-three million tourists who visit Las Vegas each year. McCarran, unlike any other, is both an airport and a casino and boasts slots and poker machines in every part of the terminal. As Mike, Floyd, and Ray made their way from gate 16 to the baggage claim area, a woman in the distance squealed like a pig stuck under a fence, after hitting a $1,200 jackpot on a quarter slot machine.

Gary Stehlik recognized the three Tucson detectives by their TPD hats and welcomed each to his city. After a brief wait for their luggage, the four made a hurried exit from the terminal and a short walk to Detective Stehlik's waiting vehicle, which he had left in the parking garage.

Gary Stehlik retired from the Las Vegas Metropolitan Police Department in 2004 after thirty years of service. He carried his position as captain of the homicide unit over to the Clark County Sheriff's Office where he had been double dipping for the past three years. Like Mike, he was an excellent detective and administrator. Physically, however, he appeared as though he had been ridden hard and put away wet. His thinning hair, doctored with Grecian Formula, looked like Mike's hair during Monday's windstorm, though for Gary this was just the norm. A fairly large and noticeable three inch scar ran horizontally just above his right eyebrow, while his prizefighter's nose had obviously been broken on many occasions. His waistline bore witness to his passion for beer, which was only exceeded by his love affair with pasta.

The trip from McCarran International to the headquarters of the Clark County Sheriff's Department was a short half hour ride that bypassed the congestion of the Strip and the downtown business district.

Clark is one of the fastest growing and largest counties in the United States. Its 8012 square miles makes it larger than the state of New Jersey, and at this point, it can still accommodate the five thousand people who arrive each month to take in all that the city has to offer. The amount of available water is the only limiting factor on this county's future growth. The majority of the people who reside in Clark County live in either Las Vegas (population of seven hundred thousand) or Henderson to the east (population of three hundred thousand).

"So, Gary, how did this case end up in your lap if the murder occurred in Henderson?" asked Mike, wondering why the Henderson Police Department wasn't in charge of the investigation and wanting to be clear on the jurisdictional boundaries.

"If not for just a few yards, you'd be dealing with the Henderson Police Department instead of me," answered Gary. "Crooked Tree Lane, where the murder occurred, is also the eastern edge of Henderson's city limit. Since both the car and body were pulled out onto the eastern shoulder of the road heading north, it was technically in the county and out of the city limits."

Gary then changed the subject. "Before we go to my office, what do you say I take you up to the scene?"

"We'd appreciate that," said Mike, answering for the group. "I can always get a better feel for a case after I see the crime scene."

As they traveled, Gary Stehlik shared with his three guest detectives his conversation earlier in the day with John Smallwood's former law office in New York, which still bears his name. Having already received the news, the entire firm was in a state of shock. The managing partner, Edward Fink, had already instructed a team of administrative assistants to begin compiling a list of all of John's past clients in anticipation that the police would request this information for their investigation. This was no small task, as John practiced law for over thirty years, many of which occurred before advance record-keeping technologies had been developed and implemented at the firm. Mr. Fink instructed his assistants to work around the clock, if necessary, in the hopes that they would be able to compile this list in a matter of days.

Highway 93, heading east out of Henderson toward Boulder City, and then on to the Hoover Dam, is a divided stretch of road with an occasional traffic light that temporarily slows vehicles down from the sixty-five mile per hour posted speed limit. The right hand turn onto Crooked Tree Lane led to nowhere, except to a small number of exclusive residential estates tucked in amongst the rolling hills leading up to the Pasaqua Mountains. John Smallwood's house was the fourth on the right, and the others were owned by equally financially blessed individuals. His neighbors included three entertainers who regularly performed in Las Vegas, two notable sports figures, and a number of successful business professionals. As realtors would joke about this area, "If you had to ask the selling price, you probably couldn't afford it."

Gary Stehlik took Mike, Floyd, and Ray past the crime scene to the Smallwood Estate so they could retrace the route the victim had taken the previous afternoon. After seeing a few of the splendid twelve-thousand-plus square foot homes, Floyd commented, "It's always nice to see how the other half lives."

"The victim left here yesterday at about 3:30 PM," said Gary Stehlik, as he turned his 2007 Ford Crown Victoria around in front of the security gate of 230 Crooked Tree Lane and headed north back toward Highway 93. After driving about a mile, he pulled over onto the shoulder of the road, stopped the car, and invited Mike, Floyd, and Ray to follow him to where the body was discovered.

"This is where the Smallwood car was found," said Gary while pointing to some fresh tire tracks that were still visible in the dry, dirt shoulder of the road.

"We suspect that Mr. Smallwood was stopped by someone he may have thought was a neighbor who had faked car trouble. The suspect's car was parked right here," said Gary as he pointed to a different set of tracks. "Our CSU made a plaster print of the tire tracks hoping to find something, and if not, it might be used as evidence down the road. But of the twenty-two homes down Crooked Tree Lane, only six had someone at home, and none of them saw or heard anything." Gary Stehlik finished the tour by speculating that this was a perfect place to commit the crime. Crooked Tree Lane was seldom traveled to begin with, and any approaching vehicle could be seen coming from either direction from almost a mile away.

"As far as a possible motive, I don't have a clue!" he said.

"The same goes for our other two victims," Mike added.

It was now shortly after 3:00 PM, and the four detectives decided to make their way toward Gary Stehlik's office. Once there, Mike, Floyd, and Ray used all of their notes from Tucson, to help Gary recreate a time line of events on *his* white board and were able to create an exact replica of that which was currently hanging in Mike Groman's empty office back in Tucson.

Confident that the Gary Stehlik now knew everything about the case and because it was 5:00 PM, which was technically 6:00 PM Tucson time, Mike decided to call it a day. Gary had taken the liberty of reserving three rooms at the Henderson Quality Court Motel for the detectives, which was just a stone's throw from the Clark County Sherriff's headquarters and half way between Las Vegas and Henderson. He gave them the keys to a county vehicle and directions to the motel. "What do you say we meet back here at 8:00 tomorrow morning?" he asked.

"That's fine," answered Mike. "That's when we start work back home."

"Hopefully, tomorrow we can get those names from New York and see what the Nevada Gaming Commission can tell us about them and our three victims." Gary then added, "Somehow they are all connected."

As the three Tucson detectives made the short drive to the Quality Court Motel, Mike said, "I don't know about you guys, but I'm as hungry as a horse. What do you say we hit the buffet at Caesar's Palace?" Ray and Floyd had come to know their captain well enough to understand that his suggestion that the three dine at a casino on the strip indicated that he wanted to do more than just have dinner.

"And maybe after that we can try our luck," added Floyd. The three Tucson detectives now had a plan for the evening.

Back in Tucson, the local news was now reporting that the Nick Trikilos homicide was being linked with another death, this time in Nevada, which brought the total number of victims in this case to three. They also reported that the Tucson Police Department Homicide Unit was leading the tri-state investigation.

CHAPTER THIRTY-SIX

THE COMPLIMENTARY CONTINENTAL breakfast at the Henderson Quality Court Motel had been fairly picked over by the time Mike Groman, Floyd LeRud, and Ray Schrader walked into the lobby at 7:30 AM. The three had awakened, still feeling bloated from having gorged themselves at the Caesar's Palace buffet, so coffee and juice were all they required to start their day.

Mike and Floyd were still lamenting their modest losses from the previous night to the one armed bandits, while they subtly expressed envy of Ray, who had left the craps table with a wad of bills. Although pressed, Ray never did disclose how much he had actually won but indicated that he had left the casino with Mike and Floyd's money and then some.

As promised, Mike, Floyd, and Ray walked into Gary Stehlik's office at 8:00 AM sharp.

"So how did you boys do last night?" Gary asked, knowing full well the three had gone down to the Strip.

"We each lost about a hundred," answered Mike as he indicated that it was only himself and Floyd who were the losers. "But that little prick won't tell us how much he won," he added, faking a certain amount of disdain for their other partner.

"Don't worry," said Gary, consoling the two losers. "You'll win it back tonight."

"We'll give it our best shot," Mike responded.

Turning to the task at hand, Gary told the Tucson trio that he had just received a phone call from Edward Fink at the Smallwood & Kuehner law firm in New York. Edward had informed Gary that a number of the staff at the firm were busy putting the finishing touches on John Smallwood's thirty-plus-year client list, which would include a brief explanation of the nature of each case and its eventual outcome. They opted to use only information that would have been otherwise available through public court records in order to avoid any confidentiality issues.

"They said that they would begin faxing in a few minutes and that we might want to check the ink level in our printer," advised Gary.

"While we wait, help yourself to some coffee. Use the Styrofoam cups on the shelf."

Outside, the chilly morning air was rapidly giving way to an unseasonably warm late January morning. Unfortunately, the detectives' work today would require them to remain inside, so they would not be able to enjoy the beautiful weather.

The fax machine inside Gary's office, as promised, began spitting out pages of documents from New York at around 9:15 AM. The first page indicated that there were 316 pages to follow. It would take over an hour for the machine to complete its task, during which time the paper collection bin would be emptied four times to prevent overflowing. This pile of paper summarized John Smallwood's entire stellar career, some twelve hundred cases in all.

The long running popular television show, *Law & Order*, portrays detective work as fast paced and exciting. After all, their "ripped from the headlines" cases had to be solved in an hour, which included the suspect's trial and inevitable conviction. Real life detective work, on the other hand, is anything but fast paced. Countless hours are often spent following false leads, conducting surveillance from an unmarked police car for eight straight hours without a break, and like today, pouring over page after page of seemingly endless documents looking for one specific jewel.

The four detectives worked together to organize John Smallwood's twelve hundred cases. They placed each case into one of five various categories: cases that John Smallwood had won, cases that were dismissed, cases that were pled out, cases that John Smallwood lost, and finally, cases that were lost, but subsequently overturned on appeal. The team took only a short break for lunch to enjoy pizzas that had been delivered to the office, so by 4:00 PM, they felt that they had a substantial handle on their task. Admittedly, their focus was placed primarily on the outcome of each case, rather than the content. Had they focused on the content of each case, it is possible that one would have jumped out at them, but for today, it went unnoticed.

Realizing they would finish by the end of the day, Gary Stehlik contacted the Nevada Gaming Commission and asked to be connected to John Bart's office.

"John, this is Gary Stehlik with the Clark County Sheriff's Department," he said.

Hearing only Gary's end of the conversation, Mike, Floyd, and Ray learned that the person on the other end was familiar with Gary from a previous encounter. "You're right, that was about four years ago. I was still with the Las Vegas Police back then."

"I'm working on a case with three Tucson detectives, and we could sure use your help," Gary continued. He then gave John Bart the details of their investigation.

After a few moments, Gary said, "Just a minute, let me ask them."

Gary turned to Mike and inquired as to how many of John Smallwood's cases had fallen into the "lost" category, assuming that these clients would be the ones who might be harboring a grudge.

To afford Mike a minute or two to come up with an estimated final tally, Gary killed time by exchanging pleasantries with John Bart.

Now with Mike's answer, Gary said hesitantly, "We need you to run about seventy names for us." Gary feared that this number might be too large and too consuming of John's time.

Mike, Floyd, and Ray let go a collective sigh of relief when after a short pause Gary said, "That'll be great, John, we owe you big time! When is good for you?"

Gary ended the conversation by thanking John Bart again. "We'll see you tomorrow morning at 9:00."

By 4:30 PM, the four detectives finished their day's work. Gary Stehlik asked his three guests if they were planning a repeat visit to the Strip.

Giving the proverbial needle to Mike and Floyd, Ray was the first to answer. "You bet! That's easy money."

"And we've got to try to win our money back," Floyd responded.

"If you guys are interested," said Gary, after listening to the three Tucson detectives sound like a bunch of country bumpkins, "I've got free tickets for David Copperfield's 8:00 PM show at the MGM Grand. They're yours if you want them."

Mike, Floyd, and Ray, looking at each other in obvious agreement, enthusiastically thanked their host.

Floyd said, "I've seen that guy on TV. He's amazing."

Gary replied, "Well, these seats are the second row, front and center. You should be able to see anything that slides up or down his sleeve."

"How did you get these seats," asked Mike, knowing there must be a story.

"I've got a connection," Gary said. "My wife and I go to shows there all the time," he added, unwilling to share any details of how he secured the tickets. "This is just my way of saying thank you for coming up here and for all of your hard work. Just pick them up at the will call window at the box office."

The Las Vegas television stations were now covering the John Smallwood homicide investigation, which they reported was linked to two others, one in Tucson, Arizona, and the other in Del Mar, California. They described the victim as "a prominent retired New York attorney and a resident of the exclusive Crooked Tree Estates in Henderson."

Meanwhile, on Interstate 10, just thirty miles west of Houston, Texas, Round Face Tony was unaware that over the course of the next few days, his murderous spree would come to a premature end.

CHAPTER THIRTY-SEVEN

I NORMALLY ENJOY listening to classical music while traveling, as I find its mathematical precision to be somehow cathartic. But after eight hours of driving, even my favorite CD's can become tiresome.

Here in the state of Texas, along Interstate 10, there is very little traffic on the long stretches of highway that connect a series of small towns. I turned off my music, enjoyed the quiet and the wide open spaces, and reflected upon my recent activities.

I feel no remorse for having killed three men. I have apologized in the past for things that I have done because, as it was explained to me, it was the socially acceptable thing to do. But my words were nothing more than words.

I neither liked nor disliked my victims. Nick Trikilos seemed like a nice guy, although he drank and talked too much. When we finished playing golf, he even picked up the tab for all of our drinks. Dominic Cirillo greeted me with a "good morning" just moments before I split his head open like a melon. And John Smallwood was nice enough to stop and help a complete stranger who was having car trouble. Although they were probably all nice guys and undoubtedly loved by their families, killing these three, to me, was nothing more than a task, not unlike emptying the dishwasher or folding laundry.

Don't get me wrong, I know the difference between right and wrong. My mother made certain of that. Unlike my dad who played golf every Sunday, Mom took her four boys to Sunday school, and then to Mass. I was raised a Catholic and have received the sacrament of Holy Communion. But I find my religious teachings at times to be ambiguous, incongruous, and often contradictory.

One of the Ten Commandments, found in the Old Testament of the Bible, is "Thou shall not kill." This is a fundamental principal of not just Christianity, but of all religions. Yet how many people, in the course of history, have been killed in the name of God? Just look back at the crusades of the eleventh century, the radical Islamic extremists of today, and every "holy war" in between. Is it permissible to kill in God's name if you are at war? Is it permissible if you are defending yourself or your family? And what about "an eye for an eye?"

While "Thou shall not kill" is one of God's commandments, so is "Honor thy father." When the laws of God conflict, which one trumps the other? Men have always killed for noble reasons. Can anything be nobler than to do your father's bidding, by taking on his enemies who have grievously wronged him? What better way is there for a son to honor his father?

CHAPTER THIRTY-EIGHT

IT WAS FRIDAY morning, January 25, and now nine days after the Nick Trikilos homicide. The three Tucson detectives were at the Quality Court Motel having breakfast a little earlier than the previous day. As the sun made its first appearance over the horizon, David Copperfield's show at the MGM Grand was the main topic of the trio's conversation, as Mike, Floyd, and Ray relived each magical moment.

"He has to have a twin. There is no way that he can be locked inside that box and then reappear in a split second in the back of the auditorium," said Floyd, trying to explain one of the magician's illusions. "Physically, it just can't happen."

"The guy is amazing," conceded Mike, unwilling to speculate as to the engineering involved in each trick. Although no one would have guessed it given Mike's line of work and his tough demeanor, the captain preferred to keep an almost childlike wonderment of magic.

The David Copperfield show, including an intermission, had lasted just over two and a half hours, which left the three detectives little time to gamble. In the short period of time, however, the gambling gods had smiled favorable on Mike and Floyd, while they almost broke even with Ray, who wasn't acting quite as cocky as he had the day before.

Just then, Mike's cell phone rang with a call from Del Mar, California. "Good morning, Josh," said Mike. "You sure got an early start this morning."

"I got the CSU report back," said Josh Present, wasting little time. "The room Tony Bianco stayed in at the Seaside Motel was clean. "This guy didn't leave a trace of anything. I'm kind of at a dead end right now. How are you guys making out?"

"We should get our CSU and coroner's reports back sometime today on the Henderson victim. We also have our meeting with the Nevada Gaming Commission at nine this morning."

Josh understood the significance of this meeting. Floyd had explained to him on Wednesday that the gaming commission might be able to somehow link the three victims together using an organized crime angle.

"Good luck, and let me know what you come up with," said Josh, ending the call.

Mike pushed his half-eaten bagel, which was stale and obviously recycled from the previous day (if not the day before) to the center of the table, indicating to Floyd and Ray that it was time to go. Floyd took one final sip of his coffee while Ray jammed an unopened banana into his coat pocket to be eaten as a snack later in the day.

The 8:00 AM shift change was about to occur at the Clark County Sheriff's Department, which created a busy parking lot at the time the three detectives arrived. An equal number of cars were entering the parking lot as were leaving. Gary Stehlik arrived immediately after the three Tucson detectives had parked, and waited for them while they gathered their belongings from the car. As they walked in together to collect their files, Mike, Floyd, and Ray again thanked their host for the Copperfield tickets and offered their review of the performance.

The meeting with John Bart, at the offices of the Nevada Gaming Commission at 9:00 AM, would leave the detectives enough time to stop by the Clark County Crime Scene Lab, which was conveniently located on the way. Having completed their investigation, the lab had called late in the day on Thursday to inform Gary that their report was ready, but this was after the three Tucson detectives had already left the office for the day. Gary Stehlik was told that he could pick up the copies of their report Friday morning or that they would be delivered to him later in the day. He chose the former. The Clark County CSU Lab was a two-story freestanding building located just a few hundred yards from the Las Vegas city limit sign on Highway 582. The director, Mike Navarro, was prepared for Gary Stehlik's arrival at 8:20 AM and had placed his file on his desk and on top of twelve others.

"Hi, Mike," said Gary as the four entered the lab. Gary Stehlik then introduced his three Tucson guests, Mike, Floyd, and Ray.

Addressing the Tucson detectives, Mike Navarro said, "Before I forget, tell my buddy Frank down at your CSU in Tucson that Mike from Las Vegas said hello. I met Frank at the National Crime Scene Unit Investigators Convention last October in Atlanta.

Mike Navarro then shocked his namesake, who was now seated across from him at his desk, by saying, "Frank is one crazy guy. He really knows how to party."

"I'll be sure to do that," said a puzzled Mike Groman. He was sure that Mike Navarro was not talking about the same Frank that he knew. He had *his* Frank pegged as a mealy-mouthed lab nerd, though a first rate scientist, who wouldn't say shit if he had a mouth full of it, although Mike admittedly didn't know Frank socially.

Handing the report to Gary Stehlik, Mike Navarro gave an oral summary of its contents. The murder weapon, a Ping Eye 2 golf club, a two iron with the serial number 14684, had no fingerprints as they had expected. The blood, which covered the head of the club and extended up the shaft, belonged only to the victim, John Smallwood. One set of tire tracks at the scene were likely made by the suspect's vehicle. The lab's computers matched the tread pattern with a 205/60R-16 Bridgestone tire, which was standard factory issue on Lincoln Town Cars beginning in 2003. The amount of wear on the tread let them estimate that the tires were about one to two years old, based on normal conditions and twelve thousand miles per year of use. Footprints in the dirt where a brief scuffle had apparently occurred were matched to the victim and to an unidentified person wearing a pair of size 11½ to 12 shoes, who probably weighed around two hundred pounds. The sole of the shoe was smooth, indicating that it was a dress shoe rather than a sneaker, but the specific identification of a brand or style would be impossible.

"That all fits with what we know," said Mike Groman. "Our witnesses describe our suspect as a large person and about two hundred pounds. The motel manager in Del Mar has a 2006 Lincoln Town Car listed on his registration form, though at the time we thought that was bogus."

After the courteous and obligatory gestures of appreciation had concluded, Mike, Floyd, Ray, and their host, Gary Stehlik, were on their way to the Nevada Gaming Commission for their 9:00 AM scheduled meeting with John Bart.

John Bart had obviously expected the four detectives, as he had moved two additional chairs into his already cramped office. His job was such that he could go for months without a visitor, other than another employee of the Nevada Gaming Commission. He considered himself quite social and often wondered why he had chosen a career that placed him in virtual isolation for eight hours a day. He would have been far better suited selling used cars, although his gimpy knees would have made it difficult for him to walk across the lot. The twenty-year veteran of the Nevada Gaming Commission, bad knees and all, was also a volunteer assistant coach for the boy's junior varsity basketball team at Las Vegas Central High School, where he had served in that capacity for the past three seasons following his son Joey's stellar career at the same school.

"Come on in, Gary," said John, looking up from his desk at his guests that had just arrived and were now standing in his doorway. "It's good to see you again."

"Thanks, John. I'd like you to meet Mike Groman, Floyd LeRud, and Ray Schrader from Tucson." Each exchanged greeting and handshakes.

"I'm sorry that it's so crowded in here. I don't get many visitors," explained John Bart. "Squeeze in and grab a chair."

Once everyone was situated, John turned his swivel chair forty-five degrees to face his computer, and the four went to work. Gary Stehlik, using the New York files of John Smallwood's lost cases that the team had compiled the day before, was eager to get started. But before he ran any of the names from John Smallwood's files, he wanted to start with Dominic Cirillo and Nick Trikilos.

Once a name was typed in, the computer would search for any link the person may have had to organized crime. John's printer, which sat on his desk and was situated directly across from Mike Groman, would deliver a print out with the words "No Match" if the person's name was not in their databank.

It was not surprising that the first name entered, Dominic Cirillo, yielded over three pages of information detailing his involvement with the Genovese crime family. The Del Mar victim, who resembled the singer Tony Bennett, was quite an infamous character. The report chronicled his ascent in the family from "wise guy" in the fifties to the position of consigliere in the late sixties and to his ultimate arrest, trial, conviction, and finally his retirement in Southern California in 1985. As the report would conclude, he was a major criminal player.

The second name given to John Bart was that of Nickolas Trikilos. Although his report was considerably shorter than Dominic Cirillo's, the name produced some information nonetheless. It revealed that Johnny "Batts" Battaglia was arrested in 1968, charged and convicted on three counts of money laundering and running a gambling operation for Joseph Bonnano. The report showed that in the course of the investigation into Battaglia's criminal activities, it was discovered that Battaglia, for two years, had wired Nick Trikilos money each month to an address in Mt. Holly, New Jersey, where Nick had become a resident. The report stated that the investigators had suspected that this money was payment for a hit on Michael Santana, whose brother Paul was the head of his own crime family and a rival of Joseph Bonnano. However, as Mike and his team were already aware, there was not enough evidence to result in Nick's arrest, even after a thorough investigation. To this day, the case remains open and the murder unsolved.

John Bart, with the help of Gary Stehlik, began running the seventy-three names from the New York attorney's list of lost cases, while Mike, Floyd, and Ray looked over the two printed reports on Dominic Cirillo and Nick Trikilos.

Suddenly, Ray Schrader, in the midst of reading the report on Nick Trikilos, startled the group by exclaiming, "Paul Santana, that was one of the names I categorized yesterday!"

Excitedly, Gary Stehlik hurried through his stack of papers. "Here it is, Paul Santana. He was a client of John Smallwood back in 1972, arrested on gambling charges and sentence to seven years in prison."

John Bart typed in the name, and within a few moments, the printer began spewing out the team's anticipated information.

Paul Santana, aka Sonny, was the head of the Santana crime family and a rival of the Bonnano, Genovese, Gambino, Columbo, and Lucchese families, which together made up what is known as the mafia, or La Cosa Nostra. From the midfifties to the late sixties, Paul Santana had tried, with some success, to take over their gambling operations in New York, but in the process had stepped on some very important and notorious toes. In 1972, he was arrested and faced numerous charges stemming from his illicit gambling enterprises. He hired an up-and-coming criminal defense attorney, John Smallwood, who had been making a name for himself in the legal community. John Smallwood lost this case, and as a result, Paul Santana spent the next seven years in the Sing Sing Correctional Facility in Ossining, New York. Upon his release in 1980, he retired to Scottsdale, Arizona, leaving behind his life of crime. Since he was also sentenced to lifetime probation, the Department of Corrections had a record of his current address as 9466 E. Maricopa Way, Scottsdale, Arizona, 85258. His date of birth indicated that he was ninety-two of age.

The report also listed his wife, Angelina (deceased) and four sons: Paul Jr., Michael, Joseph, and Anthony—none of whom had any known ties to organized crime or were ever a part of their father's business.

John Bart ran the remainder of Gary Stehlik's names, but the four detectives knew that they had found what they were looking for: information linking all three victims together and more importantly, one common denominator.

CHAPTER THIRTY-NINE

THE DAY HAD already been extremely productive, even though it was only 11:45 AM. The detectives' meeting with John Bart at the Nevada Gaming Commission had changed the entire course of the investigation. Feeling a sense of urgency and not knowing if John Smallwood would be the final victim or only the third of many, Mike said to Gary Stehlik, "I think it's time we get home. We need to get to Scottsdale and talk to Paul Santana."

"I wonder what kind of shape he's in," commented Gary, questioning the ninety-two-year-old's possible mental and physical conditions.

Mike Groman was able to garner three seats on American Airlines flight 846 from Las Vegas to Tucson. The 4:45 departure, though inconvenient, was the earliest available flight, as Friday afternoon travel was always at a premium. Because the Tucson detectives had a few hours before they needed to check in at McCarran International Airport, they decided to put their time to good use.

The coroner's report had arrived at Gary Stehlik's office while the team met with John Bart. Although the four detectives were confident that the report would not reveal any new information, they read it carefully just the same, a courtesy to the person who had spent hours performing the autopsy and preparing the analysis. Struggling with the medical terminology, Mike thought to himself, "Where is Claire when I need her?" referring to *his* coroner, Claire Pontius.

Unlike Dominic Cirillo's death, which was the result of one well-placed blow to the head, John Smallwood had numerous wounds, many of which were defensive in nature. Six broken fingers, a shattered wrist, and numerous contusions on his hands and forearms, indicated the retired New York lawyer, bad back and all, had fought desperately though unsuccessfully for his life. The lethal blow from the Ping Eye 2 two iron had slipped past his defenses and crushed his skull, not unlike a broom handle striking a piñata at a child's birthday party. John Smallwood, like Nick Trikilos, had been savagely attacked.

After finishing the coroner's report, Mike still had time available to engage Floyd, Ray, and Gary Stehlik in a game he liked to call "what we know and what we don't." In reality, there was a third and equally important component: "what we *think* we know." This was a simple exercise that Mike liked to use to clarify existing knowledge and to chart future courses of action. It was particularly useful in multifaceted investigations—like this case.

Ray, who everyone agreed had the best handwriting, put those three headings on Gary Stehlik's white board using an erasable marker. Ray began the brainstorming activity with the obvious. "We have three known victims, and each was killed with a different golf club from the same set."

Participating in his own game, Mike added, "We know that all three homicides are probably somehow linked to the Santana crime family."

Gary interrupted the flow of the game and asked, "Speaking of the Santana family, what were the names again of his sons?"

"I've got that right here." Floyd shuffled through the reports from the Nevada Gaming Commission and quickly found the correct page. "We've got Paul Jr., Joseph, Michael, and Anthony."

The significance of the last name suddenly hit each detective simultaneously, which in the heat of the moment at John Bart's office had gone unnoticed.

Putting their discovery into the context of Mike's game, Gary stated the obvious. "We think we know that Paul Santana's son, Anthony, may be our suspect Round Face Tony."

Ray wrote both fast and furiously in an attempt to keep pace with the brainstorming session. "So if Anthony Santana is our Round Face Tony, we think we know that he is mildly autistic and possibly obsessive compulsive."

Mike, now considering possible motives, said, "We think we know that Nick Trikilos was probably murdered as payback for his hit on Paul Santana's brother, Michael."

"And John Smallwood may have been murdered because he didn't get Paul Santana out of his legal troubles," added Ray.

"We don't know what was behind Dominic Cirillo's murder," chimed in Gary, "other than that he was a member of the rival Genovese crime family. And we don't know why Anthony Santana used a golf club as a murder weapon."

"A gun would have been much easier," Mike commented.

Floyd, who had yet to jump in as an active participant in the game, said almost apologetically, "I'm not sure which category to put this in."

"What's that?" asked Mike, indicating encouragement from the tone of his voice.

"If Anthony Santana is our guy, then he had to have spent a considerable amount of time, probably months and months, stalking these three victims before he systematically executed them over a one week period of time."

It took a couple of moments for Mike, Gary, and Ray to digest what Floyd had just posited. Pressing Floyd as to how he came to that conclusion, Mike asked, "How do you figure?"

"Well," Floyd explained, "all three victims, along with their ties to Paul Santana, shared something else in common: they were all murdered on a day that they each performed a weekly and regularly scheduled activity. Nick Trikilos played golf *every* Tuesday afternoon with Steve Brennan. Dominic Cirillo went to the Del Mar Race Track *every* Friday to play the ponies or buy vegetables at the farmer's market. John Smallwood had a 4:00 PM chiropractic appointment *every* Tuesday afternoon. He stalked his victims over an extended period of time. That could be the only way that Round Face Tony or Anthony Santana would know when and where to find his targets and plan their executions."

Suddenly their game ended. Over the next half hour, Mike, Ray, and Gary Stehlik could not stop thinking about Floyd's chilling observation.

Shortly after 2:00 PM, the Clark County Sherriff's detective drove his three Tucson counterparts to the Quality Court Motel that they had called home for the past two days. It took only a few moments for the three to pack and check out, and they were soon on their way to the McCarran International Airport for their 4:45 PM nonstop flight to Tucson. Along the way, Gary Stehlik, like Josh Present in California, agreed to hand the reins of his investigation over to the Tucson detectives. Because the twisting path now led back to Arizona and because Mike Groman had more resources, it only made sense to do so.

Upon arriving at the passenger drop-off area at the airport terminal, Mike, Floyd, and Ray genuinely thanked their host for his hospitality. All agreed that their time in Las Vegas had been productive, as well as enjoyable. Mike promised continued updates on the status of their case, while Gary offered his full cooperation if the team needed his help at any time in the future.

The three entered the airport terminal a little over an hour before their scheduled departure. Mike spent his time on the phone with Police Chief George Sladek, and then Josh Present in Southern California. Meanwhile, Floyd and Ray played the slot machines, conveniently located right at their gate, lucky number 21. Their desperate last-ditch effort to strike gold failed.

CHAPTER FORTY

MIKE GROMAN HAD set his alarm to go off at 5:00 AM, which he considered to be an ungodly hour of the morning under the best of circumstances. Saturday was normally a day off for the captain, but today was different. He had arranged to meet Floyd and Ray at 6:00 AM, so that the three could make the two hour commute to Scottsdale for a visit with Paul Santana.

The three detectives had returned to Tucson the previous evening, following a three-hour delay at the airport in Las Vegas, due to what the airline would only call a mechanical problem. Because Mike had not seen his wife for two days and had logged massive overtime before that, he decided to treat Jeanie to a late-night dinner and some quality time together at Café Terra Cotta, the couple's favorite restaurant. A combination of spicy southwestern cuisine, a pitcher of margaritas, and the late hour had triggered a case of heartburn that a fire extinguisher full of Maalox could not calm. As a result, Mike hustled out the door to meet his detectives early Saturday morning after having less than four hours of sleep.

Tossing the keys to Floyd LeRud, Mike said, "Here, you drive." He had planned on catching a few winks in the back of their police cruiser.

Unlike the weekdays, the normally perilous journey up Interstate 10 to Phoenix was atypically uneventful. Other than a rest stop in Sacaton, which Mike slept through, their cruise control was set at eighty miles per hour and operated for almost two hours without interruption.

The greater Phoenix area is made up of nine separate cities. Glendale, Peoria, Goodyear, and Tolleson are situated to the west of the downtown area, while Chandler, Tempe, Mesa, Paradise Valley, and Scottsdale are to the east.

Police Chief George Sladek had contacted the Scottsdale Police Department Friday afternoon, as is the protocol, informing them that three of his detectives would be working in their jurisdiction. The Scottsdale Police, in return, offered all of their resources in the event their assistance was ever needed.

Scottsdale is an upscale community of the financially secure, located just off of Route 101 and to the west of the Salt River Indian Reservation. The Scottsdale Groves Nursing Home was built on the site of a former orange orchard, which was turned into eight meticulously manicured acres that surrounded ten individual buildings, each of which was cleverly named after a particular type of tree. These freestanding single-story units had their own staff that cared for twelve elderly residents. As far as nursing homes go, this was as good as it gets.

Mike, Floyd, and Ray stopped at the administrative office where they met Janice, the weekend director of the entire complex. After the detectives showed Janice their badges, which she considered proper identification, they gave her a brief explanation as to the purpose of their visit. She then escorted the three detectives to Paul Santana's residence, walking past Orange, Apple, Cherry, and Maple, before entering Peach Tree at 8:30 AM, catching the residents in the middle of breakfast. Ramona, the manager of this particular house, greeted the officers and left the breakfast duties in the capable hands of her co-workers.

Janice, forgetting the detectives names, said, "These are three detectives from Tucson who are here to speak with Mr. Santana. How's he doing today?"

"Paul is the gentleman on the end," said Ramona, directing the officer's attention to a shell of a man who had fallen asleep in his wheelchair at the breakfast table.

"Some days he's more communicative than others, although with his dementia, I'm not sure how much he can help you," she added.

"If it is OK with you, we'd like to give it a shot," said Mike.

Sensing that her participation was no longer necessary, Janice excused herself to attend to her administrative duties back in the main office.

"We'll be finished with breakfast in a few minutes," said Ramona. "He likes to go back to his room to watch TV, which really means that he's going to take a nap. You can talk back there."

Paul Santana was born at St. Mary's Hospital in Brooklyn, New York, in 1915, which was, coincidentally, the same hospital where Nick Trikilos would enter the world thirty-two years later.

When Japan bombed Pearl Harbor in December of 1941, the twenty-six-year-old son of Italian immigrants, eager to prove his loyalty to America, joined the army and was shipped off to the Pacific Theater. Without a wife back home who needed his paycheck, like many others, he used the pay warrant he received on the first of the month to finance one of the few recreational activities available to the troops at that time—gambling. Although he was somewhat skillful, particularly at craps, Paul Santana soon found there was more money to be made, with very little risk, organizing the games instead of participating in them. His entrepreneurial skills blossomed, and soon he was producing relatively extravagant casino nights, complete with roulette wheels and blackjack dealers, which were attended by officers and enlisted men alike.

When the war ended in 1945, Paul "Sonny" Santana returned home to Brooklyn, where he applied the gaming skills that he had developed in the army to the private sector. It was around this time that he met Angelina Scordato, who disapproved of his chosen vocation, although after three years of courtship she reluctantly gave in to his repeated proposals of marriage. He gave his word that if they had children, they would be educated and uninvolved in his business, which was a commitment that Paul Santana honored.

Paul and Angelina were blessed with their first child, Paul Jr., in 1950, followed shortly by Michael, Joseph, and finally Anthony in 1956. When Paul Santana's legal troubles began in 1972, Paul Jr. had just graduated with a business degree from NYU, Michael was a sophomore at the same school and Joseph was a senior at a private Catholic high school in the Bronx. Meanwhile, Anthony was tutored at home as he suffered from what his parents described as "a number of issues."

Tragedy struck the Santana family in 1979, one year before Paul's release from the correctional facility in Ossining, New York, where he had been incarcerated for six years. Angelina lost her valiant battle with ovarian cancer and passed away on her fifty-ninth birthday. Anthony, who was twenty-three at the time, was cared for by Paul Jr. until their father was released from prison a year later. Following his release, Paul Santana and his four unmarried and unattached sons moved to Scottsdale, Arizona, to pick up the pieces of their lives, each seeking a new beginning.

After breakfast, Ramona introduced the three detectives to Paul Santana, who actually seemed pleased with the temporary diversion while being wheeled back to his room. His unit was equipped with a large plasma television in an entertainment center placed against one wall, a medical recliner with an automatic lifting device facing the entertainment center on the opposite side of the room, two small chairs, a single bed, a nightstand, and a chest of drawers. Ramona helped Paul from his wheel chair and into his recliner, while Mike and Floyd pulled up the two small chairs so that they could sit closer to Paul. Ray was left standing as the odd man out.

The detectives' conversation with the ninety-two-year-old was very brief and unproductive. He insisted on sharing some stories about Angelina, whom he insisted was still alive, living in New York, and soon coming for a visit. As Mike and Floyd were preparing to leave the room, Ray directed his partners to Paul Santana's nightstand, which displayed a collection of individual family photos of his departed wife and four sons. Although the photos were somewhat dated, one of his sons, presumably Anthony, bore a striking resemblance to the composite sketch of Round Face Tony.

"Was he any help?" asked Ramona as the three detectives headed out.

"Not really," answered Mike. "Do his sons visit very often?"

"His oldest, Paul Jr., pays all of the bills and is our emergency contact person. He lives here in Scottsdale and visits every Sunday afternoon.

I think his other boys live out of the area, although they all visit on occasion."

"May we have Paul Jr.'s phone number?" asked Mike. "He might be able to help us."

Ramona led the three detectives back to her office where she pulled Paul Santana Jr.'s phone number from her records. After thanking Ramona for her helpfulness, Mike, Floyd, and Ray left Peach Tree and headed for their car.

CHAPTER FORTY-ONE

A DEEP AND raspy voice answered the phone. "Paul Santana."

The fifty-eight-year-old eldest son of the former New York gangster had done quite well for himself. The 1972 graduate of New York University received his MBA from Georgetown in 1975, and then returned to New York to accept a position at a prestigious Wall Street brokerage house. Although he earned a handsome six-figure income, his lack of interest in this line of work caused him to dread each morning's arrival at the office. He recognized early on that he would be unable to buy and sell wheat futures for the next forty years.

In 1980, after the Santana family moved to Scottsdale, Arizona, Paul combined his keen business skills with his culinary passion and purchased a failing restaurant that he felt had tremendous potential. Located in the heart of Scottsdale's business and entertainment district, his restaurant, Don Corleone's, opened in the spring of 1982 and occupied the bottom floor of the oldest standing structure in Scottsdale, the Flading Building. The dinner-only restaurant reached its capacity every evening, which was the direct result of the fact that his establishment served the finest Italian cuisine in the Phoenix valley, if not the entire state. Don Corleone's received its first Five Star rating in 1992, a distinction that it kept for the next fifteen years.

The irony of the name Don Corleone was not lost on Paul Santana. The restaurant was named after Mario Puzo's classic character, *The Godfather*, from the book and movie of the same name. Historians of organized crime agree that the fictional story was based on the actual life story of his father's one time rival, Joseph Bonnano.

Paul Santana had a Marlon Brando—esque appearance, and he lightheartedly and intentionally played the part each night, greeting each customer as they entered his restaurant. He made it a point to dress like a gangster, wearing a dark gray pinstripe suit, a black shirt with a white tie, and a white or red carnation boutonniere depending on his mood. His attire stood in stark contrast to that of the wait staff, who donned the traditional server's tuxedos.

"Mr. Santana, this is Captain Mike Groman with the Tucson Police Department. Your name has come up during the course of one of our investigations, and we would like to ask you a few questions."

"What's this about?"

Unwilling to discuss the details over the phone, Mike asked, "Is there some place we can meet?"

"I own a restaurant, and I'm here right now," suggested Paul Santana. "Where are you?"

"We're in Scottsdale, right next to the Fashion Mall at the Exxon Gas Station."

Paul Santana then gave Mike Groman directions to his place, which was less than a mile away.

"We'll be there in a few minutes," Mike said.

Except for the head chef, the three detectives and Paul Santana had the entire place to themselves, as the first patrons would not arrive for dinner until 5:00 PM, some seven hours later.

After escorting his guests to a large booth and pouring four coffees, Paul got down to business. "So how can I help you?"

"What can you tell us about your brother Anthony?" asked Mike.

"Oh my god, what has Tony gotten himself into?"

"We don't know if he is involved in anything," said Mike, downplaying their suspicions. "We just need to talk with him."

"He has a small efficiency in Tempe, close to the university, but I don't think he's there."

"Why is that?"

"He's spent the last few years traveling. He comes home for a few days and then he's gone again for weeks at a time."

"Does he travel for work?" Mike pressed.

"No, Tony doesn't work. He has a number of disorders that keep him from being able to hold a job."

"May I ask the nature of his problems?" Mike asked, seeking confirmation of what they had already suspected.

"My brother is autistic and obsessive compulsive. It's too bad that Tony was unable to somehow use his incredible gift," said Paul.

"What gift is that?" asked Ray.

"Tony has what is called a photographic memory. If he wanted to, he could literally take an entire page from the phonebook and after a minute, give you each and every name and number in order. Trust me, you've never seen anything like it in your lives. You could go back to him after months, and he could still spit out those names and numbers."

"If he doesn't work, what does he live on?" asked Floyd.

"My father set up a small trust for him years ago. He also qualified for disability benefits from Social Security. Between the two, he's comfortable," Paul answered.

"What kind of work did your father do?" asked Mike, now testing how much Paul Santana was truly willing to share.

Paul, however, was up to the challenge posed by Captain Groman. He spent the next half hour sharing his father's criminal history, most of which the detectives already knew, but adding some unnecessary details that shocked even them.

Because of Paul Jr.'s complete candor, Mike Groman was now willing to tip his hand.

"Paul, let me be honest and tell you what we think is going on. We have a mountain of evidence that suggests that Tony may be involved in some kind of revenge killing of your father's former enemies. We have had three victims over the past week and a half who were all beaten to death with a golf club, of all things."

Mike paused, "I realize that he's your brother, but knowing him, do you think his involvement is possible?"

Paul accurately gauged the significance of this question. Mike had essentially asked him to choose between family loyalty and morality. Paul made his choice after pondering the consequences of answering truthfully. "Our father may have been a criminal, but our mother instilled in us a moral compass, teaching us right from wrong. If my brother did the things you think, it was only because in his bizarre world, he thought he was doing what was right. Look, I've never been close to Tony. No one has been. His disorders make it difficult. If he is killing people, whether they deserve it or not, I couldn't live with myself if I didn't help you stop him. But at the same time, I don't want Tony getting hurt. To answer your question though, yes, it's possible."

Like the final ten pieces of a jigsaw puzzle, the detective's unanswered questions were about to fall into place.

"So do you have any idea why he would do something like this?" asked Mike.

"All I can think is that he might be seeking our father's approval and acceptance, something that he never had. My dad doesn't have long to live, and Tony might feel that time is running out. He may not be able to show it, but he loves his father."

"How did your brother and father get along?" asked Floyd.

"My dad was always distant with Tony. He didn't know how to deal with him and his disorders."

How did he come up with the names of his targets?" asked Mike.

"Well, who exactly were they?" inquired Paul.

"The first victim was from Tucson, Nick Trikilos. The second was Dominic Cirillo from California, and the final victim was John Smallwood in Las Vegas."

"John Smallwood was the name of my father's attorney. My dad blamed him for not doing enough to keep him out of prison. His dislike grew to hatred when my mom got sick, and dad was unable to care for her because he was still locked up."

"What about the other two names?" asked Mike.

"What was the first name you gave me, the Tucson guy?" asked Paul.

"Nick Trikilos," answered Mike.

"I think he was the guy that my father thought murdered his brother Michael. I can barely remember my uncle. I don't recognize the other name you gave me at all."

Paul Jr. sat up straight in his chair as if a lightbulb had gone off in his mind. "Wait a minute. Tony may have gotten their names off of the list."

Mike, Floyd, and Ray almost simultaneously asked, "What list?"

"Shortly after we all moved to Arizona, my dad began writing his memoirs. He thought that his story had some entertainment value. Gangster movies like *The Godfather* and *Goodfellas* were popular during that time. In his memoirs, there was a list of the people that he would have wanted to get even with, although he knew that his revenge would remain only a fantasy."

"When did you and Tony see the list?" asked Ray.

"A few years ago when we had to put dad in the Groves. We all went through dad's things when we sold his house. I've got the list somewhere at home. I hung on to all of his papers."

"Do you remember how many names were on that list?" asked Mike.

"Oh geez, maybe a dozen. I can't remember exactly—it's been a while."

"Well, if Tony's using this list to seek revenge on behalf of your father, he might not be done yet. We need to get our hands on that list right now. Is there any way you can break away from here and find it?" The tone of Mike's voice indicated more than just a sense of urgency. Finding the list could literally be the difference between life and death.

Paul Santana was more than cooperative. "You drive," he said. "We can talk on the way."

Paul's home was in another upscale area known as Paradise Valley. It would take about twenty minutes to arrive at his residence.

While they drove, Ray asked, "Why do you think he used a golf club to kill each of his victims?"

"I don't know, but it might have something to do with an event that occurred when the four of us were little. My dad was a member of the Westchester Country Club back in New York. He was picked up every Sunday morning at our home by his golfing buddies, while mom took the four of us to Sunday school and then to church. After Mass, we would all drive out to the country to pick up our dad, and then we'd stop and have lunch on the way home. Sunday was the one day that we all spent together. On this one particular Sunday, Mom waited in the car, and the four of us ran searching for Dad in the locker room. He'd always shower before we would pick him up. On that day, we saw him like never before."

Paul paused for a moment as he thought back to that event, while Mike wanted to keep the story going. "What was he like?"

"He had a crazed look on his face while he was beating a man with a golf club. Our arrival was probably the only thing that saved the man's life. Dad dropped the golf club and left the country club that day without saying a word. He never mentioned that incident again. After that, Dad stopped going to the Westchester Country Club."

While they drove, Paul Jr. continued to periodically give directions. "Take a left at the next light. You are going to stay on that road for about six miles."

"Did you know Tony was a golfer?" asked Floyd, who now changed the subject.

"When we first moved out here, all of us took up the game. Tony was better than all of us, though it drove us crazy playing with him."

Mike, Floyd, and Ray didn't need Paul Santana to elaborate on his comment, as they were well aware from Steve Brennan and Mark Schenck, that Tony was a difficult person with whom to share a golf outing.

Paul speculated that his brother was a better golfer because of his OCD. "Growing up, Tony often went to the driving range and would hit bucket after bucket of balls, often coming home with blisters on his hands that had actually bled."

"Was there anything unusual about his clubs?" asked Ray.

Paul answered, "You obviously already know. Every year at Christmas, he always got a new set of irons. I think because of his disorder, a set without the number one and two irons would have driven him crazy, you know, proper sequencing and all. It was probably not a bad thing—he learned to hit those two clubs really well."

The Tucson Police car and its four occupants were now pulling up to Paul Santana Jr.'s home, with two questions still remaining unanswered: where was Tony Santana and would there be any more victims?

CHAPTER FORTY-TWO

IT WOULD BE fair to say that neither Paul Santana's Corvette nor his wife's Lexus had recently been parked inside their two-car garage. Boxes, clutter, and assorted debris were piled from the floor to ceiling and front to rear of the garage, leaving one to wonder how nothing tumbled out when the automatic garage door opener was engaged.

"If Paul Santana Sr.'s list is buried somewhere inside this disaster area, we won't find it until after my pension kicks in," Mike Groman thought to himself.

Paul grabbed a box that was barely held together with old dried masking tape and handed it to Floyd. "Here, help me make a path to those closets." Paul gestured toward five white particle board cabinets some twenty feet away that had been installed by a company that specializes in the construction of organizational systems for residential garages.

Like fireman used to do on the old-fashioned bucket brigade, the four men passed box after box to each other until a large number had been stacked in the driveway. The clearing eventually revealed the outline of a small boat that had not been visible when they began their task. Mike's curiosity got the better of him as he removed the tops of two boxes, one labeled Kite Tails and the other Crutch Tips. The Kite Tails box contained exactly that—strips of cloth knotted together that at one time had been used to provide stability to an airborne kite. What made the contents of the box even more unusual was the fact that Paul Santana and his wife Jill never had children. The second box, Crutch Tips, was labeled accurately as well. An entire gross, 144 brand new, never been used, hard rubber crutch tips, unopened in their original factory cellophane wrappers, had been deposited in this box. Prisoners on the Bataan Death March would not go through that many replacement tips.

Like an explorer who had blazed a new trail, Paul was equally excited when he reached his destination. Miraculously, the first door of the closet that he opened contained a box labeled Paul Sr., which held a manila envelope that had the word *Memoirs* written in thick black marker across the top.

"I think I found it," said Paul as he made his way back down the narrow pathway to the light and fresh air of the driveway. The four huddled together as Paul removed the contents of the envelope and began shuffling through the papers. "Here it is!" he exclaimed.

A single sheet of white paper, which over the years had slowly faded to yellow, read:

The Santana Nine

1. Vito Gatolli
2. John Smallwood
3. Vincente DiNarro
4. Salvatore Bontade
5. Dominic Cirillo
6. Angelo Palmero
7. Nickolas Trikilos
8. Michael Greco
9. Rocco Colavito

Paul Santana guessed that his father had intended a dramatic effect when he labeled the list, although Paul Jr. was sure his father never would have dreamt that three Tucson detectives would be his audience.

Looking at the list, Mike said, "We've got a lot of work on our hands. If our theory holds and Tony Santana is indeed who we're after, it appears as though there may be six more targets."

"I don't think so," interrupted Ray. "My guess is that there may be only one more."

Floyd and Mike were puzzled. "How do you figure?" asked Mike.

"Look at the list carefully," said Ray, giving his partners a chance to discover what was obvious to him.

After a short time, Mike grew impatient. "What am I missing?"

"Look at our victims," answered Ray. "Number 7, Nickolas Trikilos, number 5, Dominic Cirillo, number 2, John Smallwood."

Mike and Floyd's silence indicated that they still hadn't figured out Ray's theory.

"What were they killed with?" Ray asked his partners.

The lightbulb didn't click on for Mike, but Floyd was able to put two-and-two together. "Number 7, Nickolas Trikilos, killed with a seven iron; number 5, Dominic Cirillo, killed with a five iron; number 2, John Smallwood, killed with a two iron."

"That's right," said Ray. "Tony Santana began with number 9 and worked his way up the list. His OCD would either make him start at the top and work his way down, or from the bottom up. He couldn't jump around. My guess is that the numbers he skipped over represent guys who are already dead. All of Paul Santana's former associates by now are quite old."

"So number 1, Vito Gatolli may be the only remaining target?" Mike asked. "That is if he is still alive."

"Yeah, and if Tony goes after him it will be with the Ping Eye 2 one iron," added Ray.

"Do you know a Vito Gatolli?" Mike asked Paul.

"I sure do. He was my father's second in command for many years. He was a trusted friend that my dad treated like a brother. We even called him Uncle Vito. When my dad's legal troubles began, Vito sold him out, and he agreed to testify against him in exchange for immunity. Dad considered him a snitch and the lowest form of life."

Mike, Floyd, and Ray did not offer to help Paul restore his garage to its original condition, nor did they offer him a ride back to the restaurant. They did, however, genuinely thank Paul Santana for his help and promised they would not harm his brother when they found him. The three then left Paul's home with a sense of urgency, but not before Mike had obtained Tony Santana's Tempe address.

CHAPTER FORTY-THREE

THE INSIDE OF their police car sounded like a telemarketing call center, as Mike, Floyd, and Ray simultaneously and frantically made calls on their cell phones. Ray spoke with Computer Technology Services back at the police station, in the hopes that they could locate Tony Santana by using his credit card receipts as a paper trail. Floyd called Josh Present in California, as promised, and shared the most recent developments in their case. Josh was particularly interested in what had just unfolded over the past couple of hours. Meanwhile, Mike contacted Gary Stehlik with the Clark County Sherriff's Department who, on his day off, had been fishing at Lake Meade.

"Gary, its Mike Groman. Something has come up, and we need your help."

After explaining the situation, Mike asked, "Can you get your buddy at the Nevada Gaming Commission to run the name Vito Gatolli."

Gary understood the urgency in Mike's request, realizing that Mr. Gatolli could at best be Tony Santana's next target, or at worst his fourth victim.

"He's probably not working today," said Gary. "But don't worry, if I can't find him, I'll get someone to help me track down Gatolli. Give me about an hour to get back to you."

It was now 12:15 PM, and the three detectives were anticipating at least a two-hour drive back to Tucson. Heading down Baseline Road toward the interstate, they made a short detour and swung by Tony Santana's apartment, using the address provided by his brother Paul. As expected, he was not at home. Furthermore, his neighbors indicated that they had not seen him for quite some time. Mike, Floyd, and Ray then left his small apartment complex and grabbed a quick lunch from Jack in the Box's drive thru window and ate their burgers and fries on the run.

Just outside Picacho Peak, Ray's phone rang with a call from Computer Technology Services. Tony Santana's credit report indicated that he had only one credit card, a Visa Gold, issued through Bank of America. The most recent activity on his card established that he was indeed on the move. He purchased gasoline at a Shell Station on Wednesday, January 23, in Boulder City, Nevada—one day after the John Smallwood homicide and less than ten miles from the scene of the crime. From there, he used his credit card heading east along Interstate 10 and charged his motel stops in El Paso the same evening, Houston on Thursday, and finally Tallahassee on Friday night. Along the way, he also charged a number of food and gasoline purchases to his credit card. As far as Ray could tell, Tony Santana had just arrived in Florida and was probably still there. He couldn't pinpoint his exact location, however, because Tony's last used his Visa to pay for his motel room in Tallahassee on Friday night. But where was he today? In the hopes of zeroing in on their suspect, Ray requested that Computer Technology Services place a red flag on Tony Santana's account. Ray would then be notified directly and immediately each and every time their suspect used his card. Although Tony had paid cash for his purchases in the days leading up to the California murder, Ray was hopeful that their suspect would slip up and use his credit card at some point before he reached his next, and probably final target, Vito Gatolli.

The three detectives had just entered the outskirts of Tucson when Mike's phone rang. "Hi, Mike, it's Gary. I'm so sorry that it took so long getting back to you."

"That's OK, Gary, don't worry about it. So tell me, where in Florida does Vito Gatolli live?"

Somewhat surprised at the fact that Mike knew Vito Gatolli lived in Florida, Gary Stehlik answered, "Naples. How did you know?"

"I'm not just another pretty face," joked Mike Groman, who never really told Gary how he had obtained that information.

After jotting down Vito Gatolli's Naples address, Mike thanked the Clark County Sherriff's Detective and said, "We're heading there now, hopefully ahead of Tony Santana."

Once back at the police station, Mike instructed Ray, "Go online and book us all on the earliest flight you can to Naples."

Then addressing Floyd, Mike said, "Find me the number for the Naples Police Department, and then pull up Tony Santana's picture from the DMV and make me about a half dozen copies."

After his two detectives hurriedly left to complete their assignments, Mike spent the next five minutes alone in his office on the phone with the chief of police, George Sladek. Because it was Saturday, he contacted the chief at home and briefly filled him in on the rapidly changing developments in the investigation. George Sladek offered nothing but encouragement and support. "Nice work, Mike. Good luck and I'll see you when you get back."

By this time, Floyd had returned to Mike's office with the phone number for the Naples Police Department and Tony Santana's pictures. Just as he turned the information over to Mike, Ray rushed in and said, "The closest airport to Naples is located in Fort Myers. It's about thirty miles away. I've found three seats, but the plane leaves in forty-five minutes. The next flight out isn't until tomorrow morning. Do you want them?"

Mike jumped out of his chair. "Book them. Let's go!"

With the click of a button on his computer, Ray secured the trio's seats on Continental Flight 4456, and the three ran to the parking lot. With their siren screaming, the thirty-minute run to the airport became a ten-minute sprint.

Along the way, Mike Groman made two phone calls. The first, and obviously the most important, was to his wife, Jeanie, to inform her of his sudden travel plans. His second call was to the Naples Police Department, where the on-duty detective immediately sensed the drastic measures that would have to be taken to protect one of Naples's own citizens. He rejected protocol and forwarded Mike's call to his captain, Dave Shafer, who had been enjoying his day off. Although their conversation was brief, Mike was able to accurately summarize the entire case.

The three detectives arrived at Tucson International Airport, and Mike needed to end the call. "With the two-hour time difference, we're scheduled to arrive at 10:05 PM your time in Fort Myers. We're ready to board right now."

"I'll have one of my detectives pick you guys up at the airport," offered Dave Shafer. "It will take you about thirty minutes to get down here. I'll meet you at Vito Gatolli's place around 11:00."

Captain Dave Shafer immediately took off for Vito Gatolli's residence to offer protection until Mike Groman arrived, who would then provide him with all of the specific details of this case.

Because the three were traveling to Florida without any luggage, they were able to make it to gate 16, for the Continental Flight from Tucson to Ft. Myers, just as the final boarding call was being made.

CHAPTER FORTY-FOUR

SCHOOLCHILDREN ARE ALWAYS intrigued by the story of the Spanish explorer, Juan Ponce de Leon, and his search for the fountain of youth. If truth be told, however, his quest was actually for "the waters of bimini," which supposedly would be a cure for his sexual impotency. Understandably, teachers feel more comfortable perpetuating the traditional myth. Ponce de Leon was, nonetheless, the first European to step foot on what would become known as the Sunshine State. His search for liquid Viagra had taken him to the southwest corner of the peninsula, where the city of Naples would be established some three hundred years later.

Located on Florida's more relaxed west coast, Naples, named after its Italian sister city, has thirty thousand permanent residents. That number swells in the winter as northerners, seeking temporary refuge from the cold, fill its thirty-plus luxurious resorts to capacity. For those who want to bypass the seven miles of white sandy beaches, shallow warm water, and fantastic weather, the city also offers golf, fine dining, shopping, and every imaginable water sport.

The eighty-two-year-old Vito Gatolli was a permanent resident of Naples and had lived there for the past eleven years, following the death of his wife, Ellie, in 1996. At that time, Vito sold his condominium and took the Everglade Parkway, commonly known as Alligator Alley, across the peninsula from Ft. Lauderdale to Naples. He moved in with his only child Phillip, his second wife Trish, and their two small children, Michael and Cameron, and occupied their guesthouse.

Spry, agile, mentally sharp, and physically fit, Vito Gatolli was what every eighty-two-year-old would be like in a perfect world. Unlike Paul Santana, who he had betrayed some thirty years earlier and who was drooling into his lap at the Groves, Vito enjoyed an active lifestyle. He had just returned from a ten-day Mediterranean cruise, along with sixteen others from the Naples Senior Citizens' Center.

Most people who live in the desert would be envious of the Gatolli's beachfront property. Mike, Floyd, and Ray were no exception.

At 10:55 PM, the moonlight illuminated the waters of the Gulf of Mexico, and though it was the end of January, a slightly warm and gentle humid breeze stirred the early night air. Mike Groman dreamt of a tropical drink, possibly a Piña Colada adorned with a cherry, a pineapple wedge, and a miniature umbrella, as he and his detectives walked up to the front door. Floyd pictured Don Johnson's Sonny Crockett character from the eighties' television show *Miami Vice*, driving up in his Ferrari Testarossa, wearing a thousand-dollar Hugo Boss suit, a pastel cotton T-shirt, Italian loafers without socks, and walking up to this pristine white stuccoed residence. Meanwhile, Ray was consumed with how hungry he was. With only a bag of pretzels on the plane, his last meal was the Jack in the Box double cheeseburger and fries that he had almost nine hours earlier.

Dave Shafer opened the door of the Gatolli's residence and greeted the three detectives from Tucson. Detective Shafer was a twenty-year veteran of the Naples Police Department. The prematurely gray hair on his neatly trimmed goatee did not match the jet-black hair on his head, although the two combined to give him a distinguished appearance. If he had a pipe and a tweed jacket, one could picture him on the back of a book jacket as the living caricature of a mystery writer.

Dave escorted Mike, Floyd, and Ray from the entryway of the house through a large foyer and into the great room where Phil was seated on an over stuffed sectional sofa.

Phil Gatolli was a prominent architect with a flourishing business that specialized in the design of commercial and residential high-rise structures. The handsome forty-six-year-old, with salt-and-pepper hair, would soon be joined by his considerably younger wife, Trish, who had just emerged from the kitchen.

If Ponce de Leon had met Trish, his search for "the fountain of youth" would have come to an end. She was flat-out, drop-dead gorgeous. Her auburn hair, stylishly coiffed, outlined a model's face that was highlighted by captivating emerald-colored eyes and a gentle smile that readily exposed her sparkling white teeth. Floyd and Ray caught themselves staring at her spectacular figure, exposed by a tight short skirt and low cut top that did not come off as slutty.

Following the introductions, Dave Shafer explained that Vito Gatolli was asleep in the guesthouse, located out back and across from the pool and patio areas. An armed officer had positioned himself inside and behind its only entrance, a locked door. Before retiring for the evening, Vito was simply told that Paul Santana's son Tony may be settling some old scores, and as a precaution, the police would keep an eye on things until Tony was apprehended. For Vito's own piece of mind, the officers had downplayed the seriousness of the situation.

Phil and Trish knew all about Vito's former relationship with Paul Santana. With Dave Shafer joining Phil and Trish, Mike shared with his audience the remainder of the details that had brought them all together in the living room of this beautiful Naples home.

Suddenly, they were interrupted by a small shadowy figure standing in the entrance of a seemingly endless hallway.

"Mom, could you tell Cameron to turn down his music? I can't get to sleep," said the Gatollis' youngest son, twelve-year-old Michael.

"Please excuse me, gentlemen," said Trish in an almost sultry voice as she left to maintain sibling harmony. Mike, Floyd, Dave Shafer, and Phil Gatolli continued to talk, while Ray Shrader admiringly watched Trish leave the room.

"Tony Santana attacked his three victims when each was doing a regularly scheduled activity," said Mike. "That appears to be his modus operandi."

"Is there anything your father does on a regular basis, like some kind of weekly appointment?" Mike asked.

"No, nothing I can think of," answered Phil. "He goes to the Senior Center a couple of times a week, but not at a regularly scheduled time." After thinking for a moment, he added, "Dad goes for an early morning walk on the beach. He likes being the first one out each morning."

"Why is that?" asked Mike.

"Dad collects sea shells. During the night, the tide brings in a whole new batch, and he likes to have the first crack at them before the tourists."

"Does he follow a regular route?" asked Floyd.

"He goes out the gate behind the guesthouse. The beach is right there. He then walks down to the pier and back."

"How far of a walk is that?" Mike asked.

"There and back, I'd guess about a mile and a half," he answered. "Dad's pretty fit."

Just then, Trish rejoined the group. The four detectives for some reason felt compelled to act gentlemanly and stood up in unison while she took her seat.

"I'm sorry about that," she said, apologizing for her brief absence.

"That's OK," said Mike. "We were just talking about your father-in-law's routines."

"I told them about Dad's walks on the beach," said Phil.

"You'll have to see his collection of shells," she said, confirming her husband's story.

"What time does he head out each morning?" asked Ray, capitalizing on the opportunity to personally interact with Trish.

"This time of year, about a quarter of seven," she answered. "It is barely light outside, and he normally has the entire beach to himself."

"Did he go out this morning?"

"He doesn't go out on weekends. He claims there are too many people as compared to workdays. Do you think that is where that Tony guy may try to hurt Dad?" Trish asked no one in particular.

"If Tony Santana sticks to his usual pattern, then yes, that would make sense," answered Floyd.

"Look, folks, it's getting late," said Mike. "It's very unlikely that anything is going to happen tonight. We'll keep an officer here just in case."

"What happens next?" asked Phil.

"Tomorrow's Sunday," said Mike. "Does your family go to church in the morning?"

"We go a couple of times a month," answered Trish. "We weren't planning on going tomorrow."

"The championship games are on," said Phil, interrupting his wife. "We've got to support our Giants."

"Tomorrow we'll come up with a plan," said Dave Shafer.

"Why don't you guys come over and watch the games?" offered Phil, in his usual hospitable fashion.

"We'll order some pizzas from LaVazios," said Trish, sweetening the deal.

Afraid of imposing, the four detectives hesitated for a moment before Mike broke the silence and graciously accepted the Gatolli's generous offer.

"Thank you," he said. "That sure sounds better than watching the games in the motel room." He justified his decision by figuring the Gatolli family would feel more secure with four rugged policemen camped out in their living room.

In front of the residence, Dave Shafer said to Mike, Floyd, and Ray, "I've got three rooms for you at the Naples Inn. It's comfortable and very reasonable."

Then, pointing to an older but functional squad car, he said, "Here are the keys to that car. I'll lead you to your motel."

Before they took off, Mike handed Dave Shafer a card that read, "Anthony Santana, 2007 Black Lincoln Town Car, AZ Plates 521 MFH," and cautioned, "Have your guys keep their eyes open for his car. Consider him armed and dangerous."

CHAPTER FORTY-FIVE

MIKE, FLOYD, AND Ray slept in until shortly after 9:00 AM. Exhausted from the previous day, which began with a trip to Phoenix and ended with a journey to Naples, the three detectives were sorely in need of sleep.

Anticipating LaVazios' pizza later in the day, the trio made the decision to forego the Grand Slam Breakfast at Denny's in favor of coffee, juice, and toast at the Naples Inn. As promised, the Inn was both comfortable and reasonably priced. A single room at $69.00 a night was a bargain compared to the Naples Spa and Resort, which charged ten times as much.

Dave Shafer was waiting in front of the Gatolli residence when Mike, Floyd, and Ray pulled up at 10:00 AM. The AFC title game between the Chargers and the Patriots was set to kick off at 1:00 PM, so the four detectives decided the night before to devote this time in developing their plan to capture Tony Santana before Vito Gatolli became his fourth victim.

"We located Tony Santana's car," said Dave, not wasting any time as Mike and his two detectives approached.

"It's in the K-Mart parking lot about three miles from here," he explained. "We didn't impound it. I've got my guys staking it out, just in case he comes back to pick it up."

Ray then said, "He hasn't used his credit card since Friday up in Tallahassee. If he's staying at a motel here, he has to be paying with cash."

Dave ended their impromptu briefing by adding, "I made copies of his photo ID that you gave me last night, and we're checking with all of the motels and hotels in the area to see if anyone recognizes him."

"That's good," said Mike unenthusiastically, as he didn't feel the effort would yield any positive results. "What do you say we check out the beach?"

Rather than troubling the Gatolli family, the four used a pathway through a small park located two lots down that provided public access to the beach. From there, they turned south and walked about fifty yards, stopping at the gate that led up to the Gatolli's guesthouse.

"Phil guessed that it was about three quarters of a mile to the pier," said Mike. "It looks like a pretty good guess."

It was about one hundred yards from the guesthouse to the water's edge, where Vito Gatolli began his walk each weekday morning in search of his treasures. Following the same path, Mike soon had difficulty breathing, as his 270 pounds sank deep into the soft white sand with each step. In fairness, the other three men struggled as well. Their trek to the pier became much easier once they reached the portion of the beach where the sand had been compacted into a concretelike pathway by a number of consecutive small waves. A number of joggers likewise used the same route for their midmorning workout.

Although their plan to capture Tony Santana was obvious to each detective, Mike felt compelled to verbalize it nonetheless.

"I think if the four of us spread out every couple of hundred yards along here," pointing toward the twenty-two houses and four bed-and-breakfasts that stretched between Phil Gatolli's house and the pier, "we should be able to intercept Tony Santana when he approaches Vito Gatolli."

The four agreed as to where each should be specifically positioned so as to not tip off their suspect. They also agreed to Dave Shafer's suggested timeline for the next day. "I'll pick you guys up at your motel at 4:00 AM. The fewer cars moving around at that time of the morning the better.

We'll drop it off at the small park and take our positions well before Vito begin his walk at first light."

"The only thing we need to do now," said Floyd, "is to convince Vito Gatolli to be our bait."

Back at the house, the pregame show had begun. On ESPN, Chris Berman, Tom Jackson, Shannon Sharpe, and Steve Young were analyzing each of the day's matchups ad nauseam, although no one in the Gatolli living room was paying much attention. Vito was in the recliner, taking a nap, the boys were roughhousing on the floor, Phil was grabbing his fourth and final cup of coffee, while Trish was preparing a platter of snacks for later in the day.

The sleeping eighty-two-year-old had a full, thick head of wavy gray hair that was the envy of his balding buddies at the Naples Senior Citizens Center. At five feet six inches and a mere 140 pounds, Vito Gatolli would be no match for the younger and much larger Tony Santana if the team's plan went awry.

The two Gatolli boys, Michael, whom the detectives saw standing in the hallway the previous evening, and Cameron were two typical junior high school boys. Their constant roughhousing normally escalated to the point where the younger Michael would end up in tears. Deep down, however, each would admit that the other was his best friend.

Phil was decked out in his Eli Manning replica jersey and his "lucky" shorts that Trish had discarded on numerous occasions, only to have the exact same pair magically reappear in her husband's drawer a few days later. He believed that this combination of clothing would lead his beloved New York Giants to victory over the Green Bay Packers in the final game of the day.

If it was possible, Trish looked even better on Sunday than she had the night before. She wore a gray New York Giants T-shirt in support of her husband's team, even though she actually had little interest in football, extra tight white shorts and a pair of sandals that exposed her most recent french pedicure. The smitten Ray Schrader was left speechless at the sight of his goddess.

The combination of the boys' wrestling match and the arrival of the four detectives was enough to awaken the resting Vito Gatolli. Only a half an hour before kickoff remained, so the seven adults used this time to discuss their plan for the next morning. Vito and Phil felt comfortable with the operation, but Trish had reservations concerning her father-in-law's safety. She eventually agreed to put his well-being into the capable hands of the law enforcement professionals.

At 8:00 pm that evening, the four detectives thanked their gracious hosts and left the Gatollis' home. The New York Giants, as hoped, had just defeated the Green Bay Packers and would face the New England Patriots in the Super Bowl two weeks later. The day had been spent watching football, enjoying LaVazios pizza and Trish's snacks, and anxiously anticipating the events of the next day.

CHAPTER FORTY-SIX

MIKE GROMAN COULD never have predicted that he would find himself crouched down on his bad knees for almost three hours in a clump of bushes in Naples, Florida. Yet here he was, less than two weeks after the discovery of Nick Trikilos's lifeless body in the Bar at the Randolph Golf Complex.

Tony Santana had never returned to his black Lincoln Town Car that he abandoned in the K-Mart parking lot. The search for him at the area motels had been a fruitless endeavor, as Mike had expected. He had not used his credit card for over two days, so the detectives were unable to glean any information that would lead to his whereabouts. As a result, here were Mike, Dave, Ray, and Floyd, hiding in the shrubbery, waiting for Tony Santana's fourth target to begin his pilgrimage to the Naples Pier.

"Here comes the bait," Mike said softly to his three fellow detectives over their two-way radios. Vito Gatolli had just passed through the gate and made his way to the shoreline.

Acting as though he didn't have a care in the world, Vito meandered up the deserted beach and periodically stopped to pick up shells and deposit them into a small plastic bag. He made his way past the four detectives, first Mike, followed by Ray, Dave, and finally Floyd, who was situated the nearest to the pier. There was no sign of Tony Santana, although the second half of Vito Gatolli's journey was still to come.

It was considerably lighter outside when the shell collector finished his walk, passed back through his gate and returned to the guesthouse. Four very disappointed officers returned to the house shortly thereafter without an explanation as to what may have gone wrong with their plan.

"What do you guys want to do now?" asked Dave Shafer, referring to their plan rather than the remainder of the day.

"He's going to come," said Ray. "He has to. His disorders control him, and it will drive him nuts knowing that he has one last ax to grind, or in this case, golf club to swing."

"Are you sure about this?" asked Dave, now somewhat of a skeptic. "I mean, what if he caught wind of our operation and decided to bag it?"

Confident in his detective, Mike said matter-of-factly, "If Ray says he's coming, then goddamn it, he's coming. I vote we try again tomorrow."

"I'm in," said Floyd, supporting his partner.

The three Tucson detectives looked at Dave Shafer, who now had the proverbial ball in his court. The others' confidence was persuasive enough for him to give it another try. "Same time tomorrow?"

The early morning television news back in Tucson repeated the same story that had aired the previous evening. They reported that the detectives from the homicide unit expected to make an arrest in the two-week-old murder investigation of Nickolas Trikilos. Each station guaranteed they would deliver the breaking news the moment it occurred.

There was nothing left for the three Tucson detectives to do until the following morning. Because none of the three had packed for their unexpected trip to Naples, they all agreed that they needed to pick up a change of clothing and more toiletries than the small convenience store across the street from the Naples Inn had to offer. After a trip to the local mall, Mike called Chief Sladek and the other interested parties in Del Mar and Las Vegas. The detectives spent the remainder of their day at the Everglades National Park watching alligators in the wild, driving to Miami's famous South Beach in the hopes of sighting a celebrity, and returning to Naples, where Mike would treat his two hardworking detectives to a fresh seafood dinner at the popular Hurricane Grill.

CHAPTER FORTY-SEVEN

IT WAS TUESDAY morning, January 29, and exactly two weeks to the day that Tony Santana began his murderous rampage in the Bar at the Randolph Golf Complex in Tucson, Arizona. For a second day, Mike, Floyd, Ray, and Dave Shafer had again camouflaged themselves in assorted shrubbery and were staked out along the beach in Naples, Florida.

It was 4:30 AM, and although it was exactly the same hour of the morning, Mike could sense that this day had a distinctively different feel than the one before. Maybe it was the doubt their team had today, contrasting with their overconfidence of the day before. Mike wondered if it was their adrenaline wearing off, which had enabled them to survive the long days and restless nights since Thursday in Las Vegas. He even considered the possibility that it was nothing more than a change in the weather. Whatever it was, this day definitely felt different.

The first light arrived a little later this morning, as a very thick cloud cover had moved in overnight, causing the forecasters to call for rain by midday. Along with the clouds, the approaching front had brought a bone-chilling dampness that was wreaking havoc with Mike Groman's replacement parts. Seconds felt like minutes, while minutes felt like hours as Mike found himself shivering while crouched, once again, in a large clump of oleanders.

The porch light from a nearby bed-and-breakfast, which had been off the previous morning, gave off just enough light to allow Mike to notice the scar on his right hand. His current state of extreme discomfort caused him to recall the circumstances under which he received it. He was playing football in Flagstaff when the moisture from a late November rain had puddled on the field and turned to ice when the temperature began to plummet during the day of the game. When Mike attempted to make a tackle, a razor-sharp piece of ice, like broken glass, had sliced his hand, requiring eleven stitches from the team's physician. The wound was quickly closed, and he was able to play the second half of the game. The scar he received that November day in Flagstaff, along with the bitter cold, reminded him of this equally unpleasant experience.

It was 6:45, and on cue, Vito Gatolli once again slowly made his way to the water's edge and in moments, would begin to travel south toward the Naples Pier.

Floyd LeRud was once again stationed three quarters of a mile down the beach and across from the pier. Off in the distance, he could just make out the silhouette of a lone figure approaching from the south, walking in the direction of Vito Gatolli.

"We've got someone headed our way," he said softly into his radio, unsure of how far his voice might carry.

Floyd held his position, for what seemed like an eternity, until the unidentified person passed directly in front of him and less than one hundred yards away. It was clear that this person, now close enough to see through the cold, foggy air, was Tony Santana, using a golf club as a walking stick. As soon as he passed by, Floyd could feel his heart almost exploding inside of his chest. Ever so softly, he whispered into his radio, "He's our guy . . . He's coming your way."

"I see him now," said Dave. "Give him time to pass and then begin to slowly loop in behind him. Once he passes me, I'll do the same. Mike, Ray, I'll give you the signal when to move."

After their subject advanced another two hundred yards, Dave gave the word and all four detectives were now in motion. Tony Santana, sensing the movement around him and in the distance, made the decision to abort his mission. Without any sudden movements to create suspicion, Tony turned around and retreated in the direction of the pier.

It soon became apparent to Tony Santana that he was the target of the four approaching strangers. Tony began to quicken the pace of his escape. He had the advantage of the firm, compacted sand of the shoreline, so he broke into a half-walking/half-running pace. Meanwhile, Floyd and Dave were struggling to move in the deep and white soft sand. Floyd was the last line of defense between Tony and the pier, and he was unsure if he was going to be able to hold containment by intercepting their rapidly retreating target. Further up the beach, Ray realized that his best chance of effectively joining the pursuit required him to ignore the geometric principle that states the shortest distance between two points is a straight line. Instead, he raced directly to the firm sand and made a ninety-degree left turn and was now in an all out sprint down the beach toward the pier and the retreating Tony Santana. As the youngest of the four detectives and certainly the most fit, Ray was able to catch up to Dave Shafer in no time. Mike realized because he was the farthest away, and also in the poorest physical condition, that his continued pursuit would be futile. He instead chose to join Vito Gatolli and walk with him in the direction of all the activity.

"Tony Santana. Stop. This is the police," shouted Floyd with his Glock 40 drawn as he stood within thirty yards of the suspect.

Agitated and without any intention of heeding the detective's demands, Round Face Tony, armed with a Ping Eye 2 one iron, decided to make a mad dash for refuge. The overweight and out of shape fifty-plus-year-old would be unable to maintain that pace for very long.

Floyd intercepted Round Face Tony as he neared the foot of the pier, while Dave and Ray closed in from behind.

"Drop the fucking club!" demanded a somewhat winded Floyd LeRud, who was now standing face to face with Tony Santana.

Time seemed to stand still. Although it was only a moment, Floyd's mind raced. Almost comically, he noticed Tony Santana's perfectly round face. He flashed back to Paul Santana's cluttered garage in Scottsdale and recalled the promise he had made that he would not harm the youngest

Santana sibling. He wondered, would Tony Santana drop the club and put an end to this entire saga?

His question was immediately answered. Time, which had momentarily stood still, was now moving in slow motion. Tony Santana, swinging the golf club like a baseball bat, attempted to decapitate Floyd as he had successfully done with Nickolas Trikilos, Dominic Cirillo, and John Smallwood before him.

Unlike his three victims, however, Floyd saw it coming. Instead of shooting his suspect, the nimble Floyd was able to avoid the first pass of the club by ducking. Round Face Tony's second swing, however, caught Floyd directly in the shoulder area, which caused him to drop on the spot like a bad habit.

Tony Santana now had two choices: he could finish Floyd off like his other victims, or he could continue his flight from the rapidly approaching Dave Shafer and Ray Schrader. He had no beef with the fallen officer, so Tony decided to continue his attempt to escape.

Ray and Detective Shafer reached the location on the beach where Floyd had been hit. "I'm OK," said Floyd as he softly and painfully struggled to get out the words. "Go get him."

"Take care of Floyd," Ray said to Dave, then confidently added, "This won't take long."

Ray took off in hot pursuit of Round Face Tony Santana, who now had about the length of a football field head start. It took little time for Ray, lean and fit, to close the gap, because Tony was now, as they say, "leaking oil." Ray's swiftness and agility enabled him to tackle Tony quickly from behind, which Round Face never saw coming. Tony went down face first into the sand, while the Ping one iron went airborne and landed a good ten feet away. Ray held Tony's face firmly in the sand by pressing his left forearm against the back of Tony Santana's bulbous head. Then, Ray shifted the weight of his entire body onto his right knee, which was lodged in the small of Tony's back, and was able to quickly apply the handcuffs. And with that, it was over.

By this time, Mike, who had been with Vito Gatolli, reached Dave and his injured rookie detective. During the pursuit, Dave had called for back up and the first reinforcements were just arriving. It would take a little longer for the paramedics to make their way to the scene, as Dave had just placed that call moments earlier.

Ray waited for a couple of uniformed officers to escort Tony to a waiting squad car. After the short ride to police headquarters, Tony Santana would be held until the arrangements for his extradition to Tucson were finalized.

Round Face Tony Santana would get no closer than one hundred yards to the first name on the list, Vito Gatolli, who would have been his fourth and final victim. The only thing that he said to Ray on the beach was, "I hope your friend will be all right. Tell him that I did not want to hurt him."

During the next half hour, Floyd was being transported to the Naples Medical Center along with Ray who, as is typical with law enforcement colleagues, insisted on staying with his partner. Upon his arrival, Floyd was x-rayed and treated for a fractured clavicle.

Meanwhile, Mike and Dave returned Vito Gatolli to his house and his anxiously awaiting family. Turning the eighty-two-year-old over to Phil and Trish, Mike simply said, "It's all over. We got the son-of-a-bitch."

Trish, who had worried herself sick, began to cry as she hugged her father-in-law, while Phil genuinely thanked the two detectives, knowing that without their diligence, his father at this moment would be lying dead on the beach.

By 3:00 PM that afternoon, Mike had contacted Police Chief George Sladek, Josh Present in Del Mar, and Gary Stehlik in Las Vegas and shared with each the news of their successful mission in Naples, Florida. Floyd was later released from the hospital with his left arm in a sling and a container full of Percacets in his pocket to help with the pain.

By 9:00 PM, extradition had been arranged and shortly after that, Mike, Floyd, and Ray were escorting the handcuffed Tony Santana onto a Continental Airlines 727, a red eye, for their return flight to Tucson.

"Thank you very much, Mr. Groman," said the always courteous and polite Anthony Santana, as Mike carefully guided his detainee onto the plane and to his seat next to the window.

During the four-and-a-half hour direct flight home, Mike looked across the aisle at Floyd and Ray who were sound asleep. Over the course of the past two weeks, he had become fond of the two and had come to appreciate their hard work and skills as detectives. Understanding that the chemistry of a team is critical to its success, Mike was saddened by the fact that in a few days he would be losing his partners, as a temporary reassignment of personnel meant exactly that. He couldn't help but wonder, however, what the future might hold.

Mike then glanced over at Round Face Tony, who seemed quite content just looking out the window, through the clouds to the scattered lights below. Mike was unable to picture this seemingly polite, large, and gentle man wielding a golf club and viciously murdering three people and planning the same for a fourth. He couldn't imagine what it was like to live in Anthony Santana's bizarre world.

CHAPTER FORTY-EIGHT

I DON'T LIKE to fly. I've only been on a plane two other times, and on each occasion, every seat was taken. I don't do very well with crowds of people, packed into small spaces. I would rather be traveling in the comfort of my Lincoln, but I know tonight, that is not possible.

It helps a little that this flight is only about a third full and that we are by ourselves in the rear of the plane and next to the attendant's station. One of the police officers that arrested me, Mike, is seated next to me, while his two partners are positioned directly across the aisle from him. Mike is reading a magazine that he found in the seat pocket, while his partners appear to be sleeping.

The city lights from ten thousand feet appear to be blinking on and off, as a thin layer of clouds are passing between us and the ground below.

I can't seem to get comfortable. The handcuffs that I have been wearing for a few hours feel as though they are getting tighter. Should I ask Mike if he would be willing to take them off? After all, where would I go? I am also cold. Should I ask him to get me a blanket from the flight attendant?

I had better just keep quiet. The three of them do not seem to be very happy with me, and I can't blame them. I murdered a trio of people, tried killing another, and in the process I injured one of them—something that I didn't want to do.

Vito Gatolli was number 1 on the list, and except for him, all of them are now dead. I wonder if Dad will be pleased that I was able to kill Nick Trikilos, Dominic Cirillo, and John Smallwood. Or will he be disappointed in me because I was unable to finish the task?

CHAPTER FORTY-NINE

A NUMBER OF days had passed since the arrest of Anthony Santana. Floyd LeRud was on a temporary medical leave, the result of the injury he had sustained in Florida. Ray Schrader had donned his uniform and was back on patrol, though this time with a temporary partner. Dave Starbuck had gladly returned the command of the homicide unit back over to Mike Groman, and business in the squad room was getting back to normal. Meanwhile, the Tucson media had wrapped up their coverage of the Nickolas Trikilos homicide, and Anthony Santana's legal troubles had just begun.

Occassionally, Mike's thoughts drifted back to Nick Trikilos. He could imagine Nick as a young street thug who murdered Paul Santana's brother in coldblood. He vividly remembered how Nick looked years ago when he and his first partner, Frank Nausin, periodically paid him a visit. He could also see Nick lying in a pool of his own blood on the floor inside the Bar at the Randolph Golf Complex.

Mike Groman was never able to answer the question, "Was Nickolas Trikilos a saint or a sinner?" Mike turned to the famous line from William Shakespeare's *Julius Caesar* to reconcile his feelings for Tony Santana's first victim:

"The evil that men do live after them, the good is oft interred in their bones." And so it was with Nick Trikilos.